Donald MacKenzie and The Murder Room

>>> This title is part of The Murder Room, our series dedicated to making available out-of-print or hard-to-find titles by classic crime writers.

Crime fiction has always held up a mirror to society. The Victorians were fascinated by sensational murder and the emerging science of detection; now we are obsessed with the forensic detail of violent death. And no other genre has so captivated and enthralled readers.

Vast troves of classic crime writing have for a long time been unavailable to all but the most dedicated frequenters of second-hand bookshops. The advent of digital publishing means that we are now able to bring you the backlists of a huge range of titles by classic and contemporary crime writers, some of which have been out of print for decades.

From the genteel amateur private eyes of the Golden Age and the femmes fatales of pulp fiction, to the morally ambiguous hard-boiled detectives of mid twentieth-century America and their descendants who walk our twenty-first century streets, The Murder Room has it all. >>>

The Murder Room
Where Criminal Minds Meet

themurderroom.com

Donald MacKenzie 1908–1994

Donald MacKenzie was born in Ontario, Canada, and educated in England, Canada and Switzerland. For twenty-five years MacKenzie lived by crime in many countries. 'I went to jail,' he wrote, 'if not with depressing regularity, too often for my liking.' His last sentences were five years in the United States and three years in England, running consecutively. He began writing and selling stories when in American jail. 'I try to do exactly as I like as often as possible and I don't think I'm either psychopathic, a wayward boy, a problem of our time, a charming rogue. Or ever was.'

He had a wife, Estrela, and a daughter, and they divided their time between England, Portugal, Spain and Austria.

Henry Chalice

Salute from a Dead Man
Death Is a Friend
Sleep Is for the Rich

John Raven

Zalenski's Percentage
Raven in Flight
Raven and the Kamikaze
Raven and the Ratcatcher
Raven After Dark
Raven Settles a Score
Raven and the Paperhangers

Raven's Revenge
Raven's Longest Night
Raven's Shadow
Nobody Here By That Name
A Savage State of Grace
By Any Illegal Means
The Eyes of the Goat
The Sixth Deadly Sin
Loose Cannon

Standalone novels

Nowhere to Go
The Juryman
The Scent of Danger
Dangerous Silence
Knife Edge
The Genial Stranger
Double Exposure
The Lonely Side of the River
Cool Sleeps Balaban
Dead Straight
Three Minus Two
Night Boat from Puerto Vedra
The Kyle Contract
Postscript to a Dead Letter
The Spreewald Collection
Deep, Dark and Dead
Last of the Boatriders

Night Boat from Puerto Vedra

Donald MacKenzie

An Orion book

Copyright © The Estate of Donald MacKenzie 1969

The right of Donald MacKenzie to be identified as the author of this
work has been asserted in accordance with the Copyright, Designs and
Patents Act 1988.

This edition published by
The Orion Publishing Group Ltd
Orion House
5 Upper St Martin's Lane
London WC2H 9EA

An Hachette UK company
A CIP catalogue record for this book is available from the British Library

ISBN 978 1 4719 0581 0

www.orionbooks.co.uk

For Liz Mandler with love, and after many a promise!

WERNER WEBER
COLONEL, POLICÍA
IN DEFENSA DEL
ESTADO, D. SECTION

THE PINE FOREST sloped down to the shoulder of the highway. A wire fence was strung along its perimeter. Boards nailed to the trees warned off trespassers. The big black Mercedes nosed its way up the steep grade. Dust had obliterated the numbers on the license plates but not the embossed police shields.

Weber braked to a halt. Lizards scampered over the rust-colored rocks on his right, spinach-green in the strong evening sunshine. Nothing else moved. He had climbed the two thousand feet in forty minutes, from the sauna-heat of the city to the coolness of the plateau. The air was thin and scented. He pulled his jacket on and set the car in motion again. Around the next bend, a blacktopped road intersected the highway. A neatly painted sign posted it.

HUBERTUS VON OSTDORF   CAMINO PARTICULAR

Weber drove left into the forest. The silence now was complete, almost unnatural. After three miles, iron gates set in a solid stone wall blocked the way. He touched the horn ring. An Indian hurried out from the lodge and opened the gates. Giant cedars loomed over cropped Bermuda grass. The house across the lawns was a long untidy building with overhanging roofs and carved-wood balconies.

The layout and lines were those of a Vorarlberg manor house. Native mahogany replaced the oak timbers of the original. Baron von Ostdorf had built his home eighteen years before. The rest of the plateau had been turned into the third richest plantation in Montoro. Watchtowers spiked the distance. Beyond the sweep of the wall, barbed wire ringed two thousand acres of high-grade coffee bushes. The breeze that was moving the cedar branches carried the frantic yelping of guard dogs.

Weber stepped on the accelerator. The sudden noise of the car sent a flock of peacocks running across the grass in a blur of color. The half-circle in front of the house was laid with tanbark. Enormous stone bears guarded the entrance door. Their paws supported scrolls with armorial bearings. Weber went up the steps, moving easily. Six feet six, well built and in his middle fifties. He wore his iron-gray hair short and had black eyes in a face constructed entirely from flat planes. No roundness anywhere. His dark suit sagged and bulged in unlikely places.

A teen-age Mayan girl opened the door for him. Her braided hair was oiled, her forehead pitted with smallpox scars. Her scrawny body looked incongruous in an old-fashioned maid's uniform, far too long for her. The paneled hall had beams in the ceiling. Somber portraits stared out from baroque frames. There were more of them

2

lining the two staircases. A gilt clock ticked away over an empty stone fireplace. The girl rapped on a door. She scurried away like a roach caught in a sudden blaze of light.

The man who rose to greet Weber was a couple of years older. He was wearing leather knee breeches and a roll-neck sweater. Silver wings of hair were brushed back over small flat ears. His face was the color of yellowed ivory and he wore a monocle in his left eye. He welcomed Weber in German, the Austrian accent rolling the *r*'s in exaggerated fashion.

"I was glad to have your message this morning. I hope it's good news you're bringing for once."

Weber dropped into an armchair. "The role of Saint Nicholas never appealed to me. Herr Schulze will be here tomorrow morning."

Von Ostdorf's monocle gleamed. He half-bowed and sat down again. "Good. You'll see that everything is ready for him."

Weber tapped his pockets, searching for the battered holder that held his cheroots. A gold swastika was set in the underside of the gunmetal cover. He selected a slim cylinder of local tobacco and bit the end off.

"How about Otto — has he arrived?"

"Last night. He's in the bunker. I've shown him how everything works." There were moon orchids growing in the rockery outside the window. Von Ostdorf looked out at them. "Did you know that I was at Heidelberg with Otto's father?"

Weber blew smoke at the wall. "No. And if I were you

I'd keep quiet about it. His uncle was the only one to lift a hand for him. Orphans can be touchy about their dead parents' so-called friends."

Von Ostdorf released his monocle, catching it neatly in his palm.

"I didn't *say* I was a friend," he corrected. "I said I was at university with his father."

Weber grunted. "I'd still keep quiet about it." He paused to give full effect to his news. "A Jewish agent arrived here yesterday from Mexico City."

Von Ostdorf made a tent of his hands and leaned into it. When he looked up, his face seemed a little sallower.

"Your statements are not usually as elliptical. I take it there's more to it than that?"

"There's more," Weber allowed. The cheroot had gone out. He took his time relighting it. "Argentina is impossible after the Eichmann affair — Brazil's no longer big enough. We know it and the Jews know it. They also know that the ways of moving someone like Herr Schulze are limited. Montoro is an obvious stop along a south-north escape route. This fellow who has flown in is a professional. But he's a bloodhound not an assassin."

There was a picture in a silver frame on the table of a stern-faced woman in a stand-up lace collar. Von Ostdorf shifted it out of the sunlight.

"I'm always impressed by your insouciance, Colonel. The trouble is that these bombshells leave me a bundle of nerves."

Weber's eyes were like black river-pebbles. The baron's timidity was imaginary.

"I happened to *know* that the Jew was arriving," Weber

4

pointed out. "I'll take him into custody in a few hours. He'll never leave it."

Von Ostdorf's smile was sardonic. "Naturally. But isn't he likely to have contacts in Montoro?"

Weber took a deep breath. His broad shoulders filled the chair. "It's possible but it's not likely. I intend to make quite certain. That's why he's still walking about, a free man. Meanwhile I know even when he spits."

Von Ostdorf's face clouded with distaste. The heavy signet ring he wore accentuated the slenderness of his fingers.

"Do you want to inspect the bunker now?"

Weber was in no hurry to rise. He studied his host through the cloud of acrid smoke. Even after all these years, a meeting with Von Ostdorf still gave him a feeling of insecurity. The baron's sweater and stockings were knitted from the same fine white wool. The leather knee breeches were the color of russet apples. It was an elegant production but then the baron could well afford it. The life he lived was feudal. A thousand Indians made their homes in the cane-thatched huts in the compound. The god they worshiped in the primitive church there was strangely like the baron himself. A remote and powerful Being, stern about the law of property, indulgent in the matter of sex. Baroness von Ostdorf had been dead for eleven years. Since then the house had been filled with a succession of teen-aged girls from the compound.

Weber scraped his chair back. "I'll see the bunker."

"At your orders." Von Ostdorf came to his feet. His eyes mocked the polite show of obedience.

Weber's memory was twenty-five years old. It was none

the less sharp. It was of a young SS lieutenant posted to Bogotá as embassy security officer. God knows what he'd expected — acceptance, certainly. The friendship of suntanned girls, perhaps — of German descent, naturally. Reality had brought none of these. Reality had been a contemptuous tolerance on the part of the career diplomats, Hubertus von Ostdorf among them. The reminder had been constant, SS uniform or not, Weber was still the son of a Westphalian potato farmer.

He followed the baron through the baize door in the hall. The stone-flagged corridor divided immediately. The sound of women squabbling came from the right-hand fork. Von Ostdorf went left. The corridor ran parallel with the back of the house. A cellar door blocked its end. Von Ostdorf let them through this and thumbed a switch down. A flight of steps descended twenty feet. The temperature at the bottom was ten degrees colder. The walls were lined with wine bins. Smoked hams hung from the ceiling. The baron walked forward pointing his toes like a dancing master. The cellars extended through a succession of arches, a labyrinth that embraced the entire foundations. Pieces of furniture were shrouded in dust sheets. A mold-covered carriage harness was suspended on wooden trees. There were crates of crockery still in their original wrappings.

Von Ostdorf turned a key in a heavy steel door. An electric motor moved it back on rollers. Another door lay behind, fireproof and set flush to the walls, floor and ceiling. The lights in the brick-built tunnel were protected by thick glass frames. A strong current of air blew in Weber's face. He heard the hum of the dynamo and ducked his head, too tall for the tunnel by a couple of inches. They moved forward, their footsteps a dull reverberation. It was the third time that Weber had been in the bunker. It was ten years old and a monument to Von Ostdorf's chronic fear of a Communist uprising. A German, working for a firm of Brazilian architects, had designed it. Germans from Guatemala had installed the electronic equipment.

Weber's neck was already stiff. There was a quarter-mile to go. They were still twenty feet below the ground. A concrete shell six inches thick enclosed the brick tunnel. Ten minutes brought them to a replica of the first steel door. Von Ostdorf selected another key. The noise of the dynamo was suddenly very loud.

They were in a circular room, thirty feet across. Four corridors led from it. One was to the powerhouse and air-conditioning unit. Another to the water tanks. The third to a kitchen, shower and lavatory. The last passage went direct to the alternative exit. The place looked like a barracks guardroom. There was a pair of double-tiered bunks, a metal table, functional chairs and two large television screens. Behind these was a rack of small arms. The Schmeisser machine guns had folding metal stocks and detachable magazines. The heavy Lugers were P.I.D.E. issue, accurate up to fifty yards.

A young man dressed in slacks and a short-sleeved shirt rolled off one of the lower bunks. His rope-soled shoes made no sound as his feet hit the floor. He straightened up like a cat rising at a bird. He was almost as tall as

Weber with hair like oaten stubble. He stood stiffly at attention, his lean tanned face smiling.

Weber raised a hand in greeting. A Flying Fortress had jettisoned its bomb load over a village in the Harz Mountains a generation ago. Otto's parents had died instantly. A distant uncle in Brazil had adopted him. His upbringing had been predictable — a dedicated preparation for a part in the restoration of his country's honor. There were two thousand like him in Latin America, young men with a cause, untainted by the shameful guilt-complex of their brothers back in Germany.

Weber wrapped an arm around his shoulders. *"Ja, Otto, du wilder!* It's good to see you again!"

Pleasure crinkled the skin around Otto's eyes. "Greetings, Herr Colonel. I am glad to be under your command."

Von Ostdorf's mouth gaped as he fitted his eyeglass and looked around. He shrugged.

"I'm afraid it's not luxurious. I have to carry in every damned kilo myself. No servant's ever put a foot down here."

Weber lowered himself on a bunk. He lifted a corner of the vicuña blanket. The sheets underneath were linen. His smile was ironical.

"I'm sure that Herr Schulze will appreciate your hospitality. He's spending tonight in a fertilizer factory."

The baron indicated a telephone. "Should he need anything else, that line is direct to my bedside."

Weber leaned across and yanked the connection from the wall. "I want no communication with the house, as of now," he said curtly. He turned his attention to the younger man. "Herr Schulze will be coming in by helicopter, Otto. Sometime between eight-thirty and nine tomorrow morning. He'll bring a two-way communication set with him — and a code signal. No call must be made or received without using the signal. Once Herr Schulze is installed, you'll allow no one in the bunker except me. This includes Baron von Ostdorf."

Von Ostdorf was intent on his nails. He spoke without looking up.

"I've already shown him the bolt controls."

"You'll open to nobody but me," Weber repeated. "I want this place to be impregnable from the outside. Expect me here at twenty-two hours tomorrow."

"And if not, Colonel?"

Weber glanced at the young man sharply. Otto's expression was earnest. The colonel eased a back itch against the upright of the bunk.

"You'll take Herr Schulze to the address you have memorized and wait there for further instructions."

"You're making our young friend nervous!" Von Ostdorf's smile held under their joint blank stare. "It's all quite clear to me," he said easily. "I have no questions."

Weber took a look at the kitchen unit. There was enough food to last two men for three months, cans of German beer and too many bottles of brandy. He made up his mind to talk to Otto about it. Herr Schulze had developed a drinking habit since leaving Chile.

The power supply was independent of the house. He went back and switched on both television sets. Concealed cameras relayed their images to the screens. One showed a ring of pine trees, bright in the evening sunshine, an enclosure the size of a football field. The clearing lay deep in the forest between the house and the highway. A steel-and-concrete hatch marked the entrance to the western tunnel. Weber adjusted the controls, speaking over his shoulder.

"I want you to keep these on night and day." He swung around suddenly, jabbing at the young German with outstretched hand. "Repeat your assignment orders!"

Otto fixed his eyes on a point behind Weber's left shoulder. He delivered the clipped phrases unemotionally, indifferent to the baron's obvious amusement.

"I am an army officer holding allegiance to the Third Reich-in-exile. I shall address no questions to Herr Schulze, obey his orders and defend his life and liberty at the cost of my own if necessary. *Sieg Heil!*"

"*Sieg Heil!*" Weber repeated automatically. The baron hadn't moved. Weber was out of practice. Otto's generation was the only one still using the clicked-heel and quivering-arm salute. "Till tomorrow, then," he said.

The younger man's jaw was hard. His stance suggested anything but bravado.

"Till tomorrow, Herr Colonel!"

The two men made their way back to the cellars. Von Ostdorf stopped by the wine bin and chose a slim bottle. He held it to the light, eyeing the gold-green liquid appreciatively. He carried the wine upstairs, closed the sitting room door and found a couple of glasses. His neck was scraggy in the strong sunshine.

"*Prosit!*"

Weber's nostrils flared. The scent of the Niersteiner recalled carnival time in the Rhineland, decked streets and laughing girls, the parades. Even the memory of Düsseldorf drizzle was nostalgic. He half-drained his glass and sat down.

"Now money. I told you, each stage is contributing to Herr Schulze's expenses."

Von Ostdorf pulled a drawer open. He slid an envelope across the table.

"Five thousand American dollars."

Weber put the envelope in an inside pocket. The baron's look was oddly expectant.

"You're not waiting for a receipt?" Weber asked sarcastically.

Von Ostdorf smoothed a wing of white hair and crossed his stockinged legs.

"Only in the loosest sense. I had hoped to greet Herr Schulze in person."

Weber's tone mimicked that of his host. "Naturally." He shook his head as the other refilled his own glass.

The baron sipped his wine, watching Weber thoughtfully. Suddenly he spoke.

"You know, Colonel, I've accepted your authority for years as well as your personal dislike. What I don't accept is your mistrust."

Weber was wary. "What's that supposed to mean?"

Von Ostdorf was running his monocle up and down on its cord.

"Twenty-five years to be exact. Without ever putting our cards on the table. Why don't we do it now?"

Weber looked out through the open window. The shadows of the cedars had grown longer. The grass was iridescent under the spray from the water sprinklers. Von Ostdorf's outburst had caught him off guard. He dealt with it cautiously.

"You have me at a disadvantage, Baron. 'Mistrust' — 'Cards on the table.' *You* may know what you're talking about but *I* don't."

The well-kept teeth flashed briefly. "Come now, Colonel, of course you do! I'm talking about ambitions, yours and mine. What you want is power in a resurgent Germany. What does your trained mind detect as my need?"

Weber's eyes were steady. Strange that after all these years Von Ostdorf chose a moment like this to put his head on the block. The colonel used the ugliest words deliberately.

"You need to forget that you're a thief. That you stole four hundred and sixty-three thousand dollars from the chancellery safe the very night your country was forced into surrender."

The baron's face was unmoved. "Four hundred and sixty-*seven* thousand. Money that the enemy would have had otherwise."

Weber shook his head. "If the defense is valid now it was valid then. You denied your guilt that night. You denied it again under oath and a court of inquiry believed you. Hubertus von Ostdorf, gentleman and patriot." Weber's sarcasm riddled the image.

The baron's smile was remote. "We seem to have been misjudging one another all these years. The time has come to be frank, surely. Both of us know that the Third Reich-in-exile is a nonsense. Broken old men pursued by

12

Jews, like criminals on the run. This lunatic business of ODESSA. Youngsters like Otto grabbing at submachine guns every time the doorbell rings. Herr Schulze is no more than a dead hand waving a flag."

Weber took his fingers away from his mouth. "You must be very sure of yourself to talk to me like this."

"I'm sure of the facts," Von Ostdorf parried. "I'm only saying what many in the party are thinking. I was at the meeting in Stockholm. I know."

Weber wet his lips cautiously. It was disturbing to hear one's secret thoughts echoed in the mind of a man one mistrusted. Careful, he thought. Very careful.

"I take my orders from my lawful superiors," he said stiffly. "I shall do my duty."

The baron beat the palms of his hands together, soundlessly. "Bravo!" The mockery left his face. "You'll find that things aren't going to be the same after Stockholm. It may be a little while but the Old Guard will topple. Policy will change. The biggest enemy to National Socialist ideals is a neo-Nazi movement. You'll see our strength deployed into key positions. De Gaulle is the only Frenchman worth noting since Napoleon. First we must have a united Germany, then a united Europe. But with Germany not France as her leader."

Weber hid his sudden excitement. This was a trap of some kind. The thing was to detect who was setting it.

"I'll go on doing what I believe to be my duty," he said stubbornly.

The baron's fingers took in the sunlit scene outside the windows.

"Don't you ever dream of snow shifting on the roof,

13

Colonel? Of rain, mist and fog — slush, even! I'm a rich man, and I'm homesick. Join us and in a year from now you'll be a free man in your own country."

Weber's thoughts switched to the man who'd be coming in the morning. Intuition told him that his own future depended on the right decision.

"We'll talk about it," he said finally.

Von Ostdorf nodded. "The unlikely ally sometimes makes the best. Your good health!" He finished the last of his wine.

Memory bridged the years again. The black night of surrender. Fireworks exploding outside the darkened deserted embassy. A younger Von Ostdorf had faced him in front of an open safe with the same air of invincibility. *You make your report, Lieutenant, and I shall make mine, I repeat. The financial records were destroyed with the code books.*

Weber put his glass down. "I'm declaring the racetrack a prohibited area between eight and nine tomorrow morning. That gives the helicopter time to land and take off again. It'll be here within half an hour. I'll send a man as escort."

Von Ostdorf smiled his secret smile. "We all hear how loyal your men are, Colonel. Are you sure you can trust them?"

"I don't *have* to trust them," said Weber. "I know where the bodies are buried."

Von Ostdorf suspended his nail inspection. "I'd forgotten. That's been your speciality, knowing where the bodies were buried. Sure General Zuimárraga doesn't have one in his cellar?"

"General Zuimárraga is in Panama, attending a convention of police chiefs. He won't be back for two days. The subject is Castro infiltration of Central America." Weber allowed himself a smile.

"Your talents are wasted," Von Ostdorf said blandly. "Incidentally, hadn't we better think of a reason for your visit here today?"

Weber glanced at his watch. "I have one. You heard something about a Guevarista being sheltered in the compound so you sent for me. I interviewed the people concerned. There was no shred of truth in the rumor." He came to his feet.

Von Ostdorf opened the door for him. "Then I regret that you wasted your time, Herr Colonel."

Weber turned at the top of the steps. "I didn't, Herr Baron. I assure you I didn't. I'll see you tomorrow."

It was past eight when he reached the city. He took the loop road around the Parque Central, hitting the Avenida de Libertad halfway down to the waterfront. The policeman on the stand recognized the P.I.D.E. shield and held the traffic. Weber gunned the Mercedes across the six lanes and parked in front of his apartment building. He had lived in the block since it opened. The owner had died shortly afterward. His heirs were still fighting over the estate. Nobody was willing to spend money except on lawyers. The corridors were generally dirty. Scabs of pink stucco had peeled off the walls. The elevators worked eccentrically. Yet the warrenlike structure was home to Weber. He knew each of the ten exits, from the garish lobby to the service tunnels emerging five hundred yards away.

The express elevator rattled him up to the roof. There were four penthouse apartments. His was the smallest. He opened his front door, standing as he always did when returning home — stock-still, alert and suspicious. There was a sheaf of mail in the box. He put it on his desk without looking at it. He locked away the envelope with the five thousand dollars. The apartment was no more than one big room with a bathroom and kitchen adjoining. The outside wall was made of glass. Cane screens on the roof buttressed a selection of tubbed shrubs and climbing greenery. There was a wide bed on a raised dais. He had bought the furniture fifteen years before and added nothing since but a couple of fish tanks. Their brilliantly colored occupants flicktailed around incessantly. They were more satisfactory than a dog or a cat. Animals developed wills of their own and had too much freedom of movement.

He showered, letting his clothes lie where they fell. A plump Chinese woman cleaned house for him. She was twenty-four, discreet and versatile. One evening a week she returned to the apartment smelling of Jicky and giggling. Weber allowed himself precisely half an hour for his sexual diversions. He never referred to these interludes, not even to her.

He dried himself vigorously, wrapping the towel around his body like a toga. He walked out onto the rooftop, an unlit cheroot between his teeth. He took a deep breath, filling his lungs with the spicy smell of the waterfront. The lights had come on, the whole length of the *embarcadero* — jewels strung in the violet dusk. The white hull of the night boat to Puerto Vedra glistened beneath the arcs in front of the customs sheds.

The ship was pulling away from the quayside. Chains of tinted lavatory paper formed frail links with the people on shore. A tug was fussing at the ship's stern like an amorous terrier nosing a greyhound. The decks were white with handkerchiefs. He watched the paper chains lengthen and break. The siren sounded a long blast of farewell. It was a moment that he never tired of. He never saw it without imagining some tight-bellied stranger seeing the shore recede with desperate gratitude. One of the few who had escaped the P.I.D.E. network. Only it rarely ended like that. There'd always be someone waiting at the other end. Which reminded him — it was too early yet to move against Von Ostdorf. The baron had friends in low places.

He went inside and sat at his desk. A match first to light the cheroot, then a piece of office stationery. He fed it into the electric typewriter and hit the keys.

> Gavilan y Compañía
> Fuente de las Mujeres L5
> Ciudad de Montoro
> D.F.
> Your reference: HS/gdr

Burkhardt Brothers
Import and Export
1164 Yonge Street
Toronto, Ontario

DEAR SIRS,

I refer to your recent order for two tons of Grade-A Highland coffee beans. We wish to confirm that the price is as quoted F.O.B. port of Montoro. This consignment will be shipped via Galveston, Texas, arriving in Halifax, Nova Scotia, about 18th. We forward our *pro forma* invoice and statement of account under separate cover.

Very truly yours,
GAVILAN Y COMPAÑÍA

He slammed a rubber-stamp signature at the bottom of the page and sealed the envelope. He picked up the phone, grunting as he recognized the voice at the other end.

"Moreno, about this man Asher! Pick him up in his hotel at seven o'clock tomorrow morning. Hold him at headquarters. No visitors, no communications with anyone."

He hung up and glanced at his watch. Ten minutes to nine. Carmen Soong would be there in a few minutes. He put a Schubert LP on the record player, lay down on the bed and closed his eyes.

The cortege of police jeeps reached the Plaza Mayor just after nine o'clock the next morning. It slowed for the top-heavy buses unloading in front of the terminal. Weber viewed the scene with a professional eye. Women thronged the entrances of the fruit and fish markets. Hotel touts were pestering the passengers streaming from the station. Traffic cops moved in on truck drivers who bulldozed the mule carts in turn. Everything was normal. He spoke sharply to his driver. The leading jeep sliced through the crowd, its siren shrill. The cortege scattered

the pedestrians, circled the bullring and entered the
narrow street. It climbed the hill in close formation, windows and shutters rattling behind it.

D Section headquarters were in the old Bishop's Palace,
a rambling collection of baroque buildings on top of the
hill. Weber climbed out stiffly. He was wearing the same
shapeless suit with bulging pockets. A razor nick had bled
onto his shirt collar. An enormous fountain spouted water
in the cobbled courtyard. There were three wings, separated by drowsy gardens, joined by cloistered walks.

He walked the fifty yards to his office, thinking of a pil-
grimage he had made ten years before to an estate near
the Chile-Argentine frontier. Forgotten faces had reappeared in the smoke of the barbecue pits. Old comrade-
ships had been renewed. And moving among his guests,
like a jovial tavern keeper, the bullnecked figure of their
host. The man who had landed in the helicopter three
quarters of an hour ago was bent, defeated and unshaven.
It was the fear in his eyes that had shocked the colonel
more than anything. He'd be in the bunker by now, the
helicopter on its way back to Salvador. There were eight
days before the next stage in the long journey north
started. Eight days in the company of an impressionable
youngster. Otto would have to be warned. The word was
distasteful but what else . . . even Von Ostdorf's assessment of their visitor's future role seemed optimistic now.
What German worthy of the name would rally to a man
lost to personal dignity.

Weber opened the door of a cool, high-ceilinged room
with large windows. Pigeons strutted across the grass out-

side. The walls were completely bare. A black-painted safe stood behind the desk. He threw his jacket at a chair and sat down. A canvas property sack lay on the blotter. He touched the label thoughtfully and opened the sack. There was some money, a few hundred dollars, most of it in Swiss and German bills. A cheap automatic watch, a pen and a passport.

Weber flicked through the pages of the identification document. It was American and false. The name given was Philip Asher, teacher of languages, born in Cleveland, Ohio, February 1938. No distinguishing marks or peculiarities were listed. Wrong there, thought Weber. The picture on the opposite page showed a studious-looking man with spectacles. The colonel tossed the sack in a drawer and spoke into the intercom box. The man who came in had thin hair and wore a shoddy black suit. The funereal effect was heightened by a black tie and furtive smile. He managed to say good morning and excuse himself in the same breath. Weber tapped the drawer. "Is this all he had?"

Moreno nodded. "That and a few things in his suitcase. Those are the only papers and there were no weapons."

Weber knuckled through his short gray hair. "You searched him thoroughly?"

Moreno allowed himself a thin smile. "We arrested him in the bath, Colonel. He offered no resistance. After the first couple of minutes he refused to speak. I've got him in the stable block."

Weber spat the end of a cheroot into the trash basket. "I'll see him later." The other man was strangely hesitant.

"Well for crissakes what is it, man?" Weber demanded.

Moreno moved a deprecating hand. "It's Flores, Colonel. He's in my office. He was on the racetrack detail with Galiana. It seems that they intercepted a man this morning — a foreigner with a camera. Flores thought he should report it."

"Where is the man?" snapped Weber.

Moreno's voice was apprehensive. "They let him go, Colonel."

The steadiness of his own answer surprised Weber. "A foreigner with a camera and they let him go!"

"They have his name and address," Moreno put in quickly. "A Canadian called Macneil living in Almirón. I've checked with Alien Control. He's a resident. They're sending his file over. Do you want to see Flores, sir?"

"I want to see both of them." Weber walked to the window rather than let his aide see his face. He had jumped the gun with Asher. The Jew should have been allowed to make his contact.

Two men filed in. Their expressions were nervous. Weber looked at them dispassionately. Both faces were vaguely familiar.

"Which of you is Flores?"

The man with gold teeth shuffled his feet. "Senor Coronel."

"How many years service?"

Flores ducked his head. "Eight, Senor Coronel. Sergeant, first-class."

"Private, second-class," Weber amended. "And you?"

The copper-skinned man with Indian features stank like

a goat. "Six years, Colonel. Private, first-class." He waited stolidly for judgment.

"Second-class," Weber said in a level tone. He took his chair, slamming his hand down on the desk. Both men jumped. "Are you both insane or what?"

Rivulets of sweat were running down Flores' forehead. He stammered his excuse.

"His papers were in order, Colonel. It was only afterward that I thought . . ."

"Report to the guardroom," Weber said curtly. "You're both suspended till further orders." He yanked the adjoining door open. "Am I going to have to wait all day for that file?"

Moreno sprang up, holding out a buff folder. The two men behind him were suddenly active with their deskwork. Weber kicked the door shut. The implications stretched his mind till it ached. A man with a camera. The helicopter with him standing there in full glare of sunlight. Ten minutes afterward he was on his way down to the police launch.

DOUGAL MACNEIL

I‍T WAS eight A.M. and the climbing sun struck the center of the city. Overloaded streetcars rattled down the Avenida de Libertad, the outside passengers clinging like leeches. The wide avenue descended from the palace gates to the embarcadero. Horn-happy motorists barreled down the six-lane highway. Banks of tropical flowers in shaded walks showed through the misty spray from the fountains. The waterfront came suddenly, the buildings taller as if squeezed by the five hills that supported the city. Tattered coconut palms lined the dusty embarcadero. When the wind was right, the smell of the jungle was strong from the estuary nine miles away.

At the bottom of the avenue was a concourse that housed the main exits from the city. Railroad station, bus and port terminals, the ferry landings. Over on the west side were the bullring and fish market. Giant diesel trucks were parked among fly-ridden burros hidden under their pack loads. Knots of cops, sinister in dark glasses, lounged in front of the coffee stands by the customs sheds.

Dust swirled about their highly polished boots. There was a hoarding behind them, the printed slogans in Spanish and English.

WELCOME TO MONTORO, JEWEL OF THE CARIBBEAN
ONE FAITH!   ONE PEOPLE!   ONE LIBERATOR!

The Rio Verde snaked through the suburbs, emptying itself in the distant estuary. Tidal water flushed the sewers, ebbed back to the ocean, leaving the fishermen's shacks encrusted with salt. Once a year regularly, flood-water deposited alligators in unlikely places. Behind the five hills were the rice paddies and sugarcane plantations. The source of the river rose twenty-three miles west in the craggy fastness of the Sierra Araña. South of the city, the radio and television beacons posted the way to a plateau. The Jockey Club pennant fluttered there, high on a mast above the white-painted grandstands.

Macneil ducked under the barrier and crossed the dirt gallop to the grass infield. The platform in front of him supported the photo-finish unit. He climbed up the steps awkwardly, the Rolleiflex swinging around his neck. His shirt was wet already. Both grandstands and pari-mutuel booths lay deserted in the gathering heat. Short sharp shadows etched the outline of the empty parade paddock. A white jeep crossed the back straight as he climbed, a cloud of dust a half-mile away.

He leaned against the edge of the platform and checked his light meter. He fed a roll of color film into the camera. He was about six feet tall, in a blue cotton shirt and well-washed jeans. Sun-streaked gray hair topped lazy blue eyes. He could have been anything between thirty-five and forty. He stared into the viewfinder, concentrating. The dark green of the distant rice paddies showed on the tiny screen. The thin white line dividing them was the Presidential Causeway. He shot three frames, shifting the lens each time to obtain a panoramic effect. He lit a cigarette. Twenty past eight. Pilar would sleep on until ten. Not that she hadn't always done just that but she had the coming baby to justify her now.

He exposed one film, sealed it in tinfoil and reloaded the camera. Fair enough. A thousand words written in the cool of the evening and he'd be a couple of hundred bucks richer. His mind jumped ahead to Pilar swinging in the patio hammock, water splashing in the small fountain, the tall frosted glass on his work table. He'd leave the article untitled. Vance would change it anyway. He wondered how much longer he could go on digging in the same vein. Mayan remains, man-eating alligators, the fascination of the Montorosan scene.

He turned sharply, hearing the chopping sound of a motor. A helicopter was dropping out of the azure sky. It hovered over the far side of the track. Another police jeep joined the first, racing to the outfield as the machine came in to land. Macneil shot the rest of the film — the helicopter added to the contrast. He climbed down from the platform and took off his huaraches. He crossed the track in bare feet, toes sinking through the crust into the soft moist earth beneath. Pilar and he hadn't been up here in weeks and they both enjoyed it. He decided to make it Sunday. They could have dinner in the clubhouse, watching the half-bred horses race under arcs in the mauve dusk. His mouth watered at the thought of giant prawns fried with fresh pineapple, beer from the German brewery, iced and golden. He wiped his feet on the backs of his jeans, put his sandals on again and walked around behind the grandstands.

The Volkswagen was in the shade of the pari-mutuel board. Ten minutes in the sun, even at that hour, and the seats were agony to sit on. He put his key in the lock, then backed up hastily. Two men stepped from the doorway of a pay-out booth. The taller had a gun in his hand. Macneil raised his hands above his head. The smaller man had a pure Indian face. He tapped Macneil's chest with the barrel of yet another gun. His gold-filled mouth shaped the familiar form of address with authority.

"*Policía. Dónde va?*"

Macneil kept his arms high. Instinct told him these were no ordinary cops. He answered guardedly.

"Home, señor."

The barrel of the gun shifted a little. It was directly in front of Macneil's heart.

"Papers!"

"Si, señor." Macneil's voice cracked a little. The squat man ran his fingers over Macneil's body with expert touch. Lizard eyes glittered in his dark expressionless face as he located the wallet. He gave it to his companion. The taller man tipped the contents onto the roof of the Volkswagen. He spread them out. A little money, driver's license. The green cover of Macneil's identity card bore a yellow stripe. The cop glanced up.

"*Inglés? Aleman?*"

"Canadian." Macneil lowered his arms cautiously. He was on the point of saying that he had a resident's permit but thought better of it.

The cop poked wallet and contents back at him; he dropped the gun in his pocket casually. It made one more bulge in the shapeless jacket.

"A photographer, señor?"

Macneil nodded. The questions were pointless. It was all there on his identity card. He lit a cigarette, offering the pack to each man in turn. Both refused. He sensed the need for a fuller explanation.

"I'm writing an article for a foreign magazine, señores. They have asked me to supply photographs. The view of the city is startling up here. It's the best time of the day for lighting contrasts."

The dark-skinned cop looked puzzled. His partner sucked a back tooth and spat.

"How did you get onto the hippodrome? The gates were shut — didn't you see that?"

Macneil picked at the end of his cigarette. The coarse sweet tobacco was unraveling as usual.

"I saw it. But it didn't mean anything to me. I didn't realize I wasn't supposed to be here. I went around through the horse barns."

The bank of gold teeth flashed. "But you hid your car!"

"Hid?" expostulated Macneil. "It was in the shade — out of the heat."

The helicopter was taking off again. The sound seemed to decide the man. He jerked the door of the Volkswagen open and gestured Macneil inside.

"*Vaya, hombre! Vaya!*" he said impatiently.

The Canadian gunned the small car past the paddock and around to the horse barns. The big doors were still wide. He had a brief glimpse of the cool interior, the movement of animals. A couple of exercise saddles lay in the dirt outside. There were no handlers in sight. He turned onto the lane that led back to the highway. He braked at the junction and glanced up in his driving mirror. Four police jeeps were coming through the entrance gates half a mile away. He stayed where he was. It took him five matches to light a cigarette. The jeeps barreled by. Each was filled with plainclothesmen. He watched them go with an angry feeling of relief. It was ten minutes before he restarted the Volkswagen. He drove fast, avoiding the holes that gaped in the road. The steep banks of the arroyo were brilliant with oleander.

It was half-past nine when he turned onto the marginal highway. At this point it was no more than a strip of hardtop covered with a film of sand. Beyond was an endless beach where green coconut palms grew to the edge of the warm shallow water. Flamingos stalked there, indifferent to the noise of the passing car. The beach narrowed after a couple of miles. Refuse from the fishermen's huts scabbed the coarse yellow sand. Swamps extended on the other side of the highway. An evil-looking mat of vegetation screened the mud and brackish water. Much of what lived there was deadly.

The highway ran straight to Montoro, bypassing the southern headland. He wheeled right. Geraniums grew like trees, the leaves and flowers dull with the dust raised by passing traffic. A canvas-topped ferry linked the village ahead with the city. An arbitrary service had helped Almirón to resist assimilation. Macneil drove into a web of narrow streets. The church that dominated the central plaza was a simple white building three hundred years old. The cart standing in front carried a sign reading POLICÍA URBANA. Both the mule and the driver were fast asleep.

The chanted responses of unseen children drifted through the windows of the nuns' school. He turned onto a narrow street circling the edge of the headland. There were no sidewalks. Squat white houses overlooked the ocean. Water ran over cobblestones to a spectacular sortie in the retaining wall. Fish heads and banana skins cascaded into the air. Waiting gulls wheeled, striking with unerring judgment. He parked in front of windows veiled by bougainvillea. The big door to the patio was open. The air was rich with the compounded smell of coffee and oil-fried peppers. Tia Ana was in her customary place thirty yards away, a huddle of clothing rusty-black against the dazzling whitewash. She was eighty-seven. They carried her out each morning, propping her on a chair in the sunshine. She sat there till late afternoon, her desiccated head hooded in a shawl, liver-spotted hands folded. He had never seen her move or speak.

He took his camera from the glove compartment and walked through the gate. It was cool even at the height of summer. The breeze blew straight off the sea. The house was built around the patio. Five rooms opened onto a covered veranda. Those nearest the street were never used. The somber black furniture there, the family silver, were part of what his father-in-law had called "the reluctant dowry." Don Estevan had taken his daughter's marriage to a foreigner as a personal affront — an unnatural alliance doomed to God's disapproval. "One hopes that you will eat," he had said at the wedding. His silence since then had been absolute.

A string hammock slung between two banana trees was fat with cushions. A tiny jet of water spouted into a stone basin. Once the maid had gone, the big outer door shut tight, Pilar and he would lie there naked, hand in hand, staring up at an unbroken sky.

He peered around the kitchen door. A dark-skinned girl with black braided hair was beating a tortilla mixture in a bowl. Her flowered cotton dress was hitched up between her legs, giving the effect of pantaloons.

"La señora?" he asked.

She continued to beat the egg mixture, lifting her shoulder. Like all of her tribe, she was reluctant to express an opinion. He opened the bedroom. Light streamed through the enormous window that occupied most of the outside wall. The view beyond it was startling. The sweep of the bay, the white city straddling the hills. There was a forty-foot drop to the plumed ocean below.

His wife stirred in the wide bed, raising her arms and yawning. He put his mouth to hers. The bed smelled of sleep and Nina Ricci.

He looked at his watch. "You planning on getting up this morning?"

She pulled him down beside her and struggled upright. Her convent English had acquired his vowel sounds. Her eyes and mouth mocked him gently.

"I am a pregnant woman."

He shook his head at her. "You've been in bed for thirteen hours. What's more you look like a shaggy dog." He took a hand mirror from the table and held it in front of her.

She pushed the hair back from her forehead. Her tan was richer than his, her hair a dark chestnut. Wide green eyes were set in a wedge-shaped face. Her mouth was on the large side.

"Did you take some good pictures?"

He rolled over on his back, imprisoning her in his arms. "The best. And you want to hear something funny — I got myself picked up by P.I.D.E. after all these years."

She struggled to turn around and look at him. "You're not supposed to say things to frighten me."

He smoothed the soft hair on the back of her neck. "There's nothing to be scared of. There were cops all over the hippodrome. I just didn't see them. They'd sealed the place off — you know the way they do. A couple of them jumped me as I was leaving. They wanted to know what I was doing there."

She broke his hold, twisting her head around. "And then?"

He smiled. "I never argue with men carrying guns. We had a little chat about things in general then they let me go."

She swung her feet to the carpet. She was eight months pregnant and showed it.

"I hate you when you're being facetious."

He held up both hands in surrender. By the time he had showered and changed she was fully dressed. He knelt

31

down to fasten her sandals for her. Then he stood and took her chin in his palm.

"I've got to take those films into the city. Is there anything you want?"

She shook her loose hair back and tied it with a ribbon. "If you see mangoes, buy," she decided. "I feel like."

He smiled at her fondly. There were times when her syntax went to hell.

"If you feel like, I buy."

She made a face at him and vanished through the kitchen door.

He left the Volkswagen outside the Central Station. The old bullfighter in the wheelchair sold him a parking voucher. A horn in the spine had left him partially paralyzed. The card around his neck proclaimed past glories.

THE SPLENDOR OF LIMA! HERO OF RONDATAFA!

The usual complement of bums loitered around the entrance to the Edificio Bolivar. The pimps who worked the bus depot; a public scribe in carpet slippers, a collection of ball-points stuck in his hatband; lottery vendors and frontón gamblers. He pushed through and climbed the steps. The lobby echoed with taped music. The mezzanine floor was ringed with offices. A sign over one identified it as the

AVENIDA TRAVEL BUREAU   ENGLISH SPOKEN
OFFICE HOURS 10–2   4–8

A globe was revolving in the window. Macneil shoved the door. A large fan turned in the ceiling. The draft from it lifted the papers on two desks. A spectacled girl with acne was rattling on a typewriter. The bald-headed man behind the counter nodded at Macneil. His nylon shirt-sleeves were caught in elastic armbands. He wore a green visor over irascible red eyes. The effect was that of a Western Union operator in an old-fashioned movie.

"Be right with you," he said shortly. He returned his attention to the woman in front of him.

Macneil lowered himself into a cane chair. He watched the performance with secret amusement. The quality of Fletcher's patience was a fair gauge of the business he was doing. He was treacle-sweet when things were bad. Right now, the flat midwestern voice cut through the woman's inquiries like a hot fly through butter. Things had to be good.

"That's *right*, madam. One boat a day. It leaves at twenty hours from the terminal across the way. It gets you into Puerto Vedra at six in the morning. You'll need an exit permit to leave Montoro. You apply for that in the *juzgado*, third floor, first left."

He poised his pen over the stack of steamship tickets. His customer wore a white linen suit, dinky little shoes with plastic flowers, a brief veil over mauve-rinsed hair. She looked at Fletcher through harlequin spectacles.

"An *exit permit!* You must be joking. I'm an American citizen."

Fletcher swiveled his long head, closing an eye for Macneil's benefit.

"That's no special recommendation hereabouts. You *still* need an exit permit. It'll cost you seventy-five pesos and you take two passport-size photographs with you."

The woman pointed a finger at him accusingly. "I don't like your attitude any too much. And don't you forget for one minute that you booked me into that hotel. I haven't had a night's sleep since I got here. Fresh waiters and roaches in the bathroom!"

"Waiters in the bathroom?" Fletcher pushed his visor up, affecting incredulity. He dropped the pose and leaned forward. "Let me tell you something, madam. You've been in here four times already this week, asking the same foolish questions. If you don't like the service why not try somewhere else?"

Macneil's magazine rustled in the sudden silence. The woman glared at him.

"How about the planes?" she demanded.

"I've told you that, too," Fletcher answered. "There's one flight a day to Puerto Vedra. It leaves in forty minutes' time. And it's booked solid for the next ten days. You'd better make your mind up. Do you want a ticket on the boat or not?"

"You *rude* man," she snapped. "The sooner I'm out of this godforsaken country the better. I want a ticket for tonight, first-class."

Fletcher's long yellow teeth showed in a smile of melancholy pleasure.

"Second-class. There's no space in first."

She unfastened her handbag and took out her wallet. *"What* did you say your name was?" Her tone was cloying.

Fletcher's thumb pinned her money to the counter.

"Charles Amnesty Fletcher," he said dangerously. "And if you want to see the management, it's me."

She looked him up and down, her nose thin with anger. The door slammed shut behind her. The girl went on typing, her jaws chewing steadily. Fletcher drew a deep breath, wagging his head at Macneil.

"What's with the grin?" he challenged. "My arteries hardening by the minute and you sit there with a silly grin on your face."

Macneil made a long arm, dropping the small package on the counter. "What's your complaint, I was with you in spirit. Take care of this for me, will you?"

Fletcher sniffed suspiciously, reading the address out loud. "*Fotos Janes, Calle Larios, Puerto Vedra.* Jesus, not that again!"

"It's color," Macneil explained. "I've got a deadline on a story and you know the sort of work they turn out here. Nail parings fused to the negatives and blue comes out the color of your pretty nose."

Fletcher juggled the package, shaking his head. "I don't know why I stick my neck out for you. I told you before, there's a penalty for sending anything out of the country except by authorized channels. It's two years on the rock pile and five thousand pesos fine."

Macneil indicated the girl with his eyes. "Doesn't she speak any English?"

Fletcher's expression was sour. "Not at this time of the morning. It's too early for her. Tell me why I do it?" he repeated.

Macneil shrugged. "You love me, Charles. I let you

cheat at poker and Pilar cooks you meatballs. They'll have the films back to me on Monday. OK?"

"It's got to be OK," Fletcher said sadly. "You're an extortionist as well as a mind reader. This beautiful child's just on her way to the airport." He threw the films together with some papers in a large manila envelope. He spoke to the girl in Spanish. "Leave this at the flight-departure desk. It's for Captain Lopez. And don't forget to bring those custom clearances back with you!"

She dropped her typing immediately, examined herself in a hand mirror and clicked down to the lobby below. Fletcher looked at the clock. He slipped the elastic bands from his arms and exchanged his visor for a dirty straw hat.

"It's almost noon. Have you got time for a beer?"

Macneil rose to his feet. "Sure I've got time. I just want to pick up some mangoes on the way."

Fletcher lowered the window shades. He turned around, blinking. *"Mangoes?"*

The Canadian followed him through the door. "That's right — it's Pilar. Last week it was smoked trout at eighty-five pesos a two-ounce can. The doctor says it's normal."

"I've *been* a father," Fletcher said bleakly.

They went out into the torrid heat. A police launch was scything away from the dock, its powerful motors churning the water. The eagle-embroidered pennant streamed out from the stern. The two men passed in front of the hoarding. Fletcher glanced up, his eyes reverent.

"One people, one faith, one liberator," he said piously. "Amen. And you can quote me on that."

They crossed the concourse to a building overlooking

the Parque Central. The enormous plate-glass front mirrored the plane trees and shimmering water. Fletcher
found a couple of corner seats and ordered. The girl
brought dishes of raw fish doused with fresh lime juice.
They were served with the tall steins of beer. The surrounding tables in the air-conditioned cafeteria were occupied by students. They lolled in pairs, young men and
girls, supercilious over their notebooks. Fletcher wiped
his pendulous nose on the back of his hand.

"Look at 'em," he said scathingly. "They come in here
and coast for four hours on a coke or a coffee. I don't
know why the management allows it."

Macneil raised his glass in salute. "It adds tone. Listen,
Charley. Didn't you once have trouble with P.I.D.E.?"

Fletcher wiped his mouth. "That was a long time ago,"
he said carefully. "A long, long time ago — before I got
religion. Why?"

Macneil batted away a fly. "Nothing, really. I mean I
don't suppose it's anything. I got myself picked up by
P.I.D.E. this morning. On the racetrack at eight o'clock. I
didn't realize it but the whole place was under wraps.
This pair got me on the way out. They wanted to know
what I was doing up there."

"Well that figures." Fletcher's voice was oddly quiet.
"Eight o'clock in the morning, you're not timing the favor-
ite. What *were* you doing?"

"Shooting some color film." Macneil considered his
nails.

The travel agent's body stiffened. He looked like a man
who has seen his own ghost.

"The film you just gave me?"

37

"That's right." Macneil tried to pacify him. "Look, Charley, I'm here, aren't I? There's nothing to worry about. They didn't even look at my camera. Salute, salute. *Vaya con Dios!*"

Fletcher leaned forward, lowering his voice to an accusing whisper. "You knew that plane leaves at noon. Those films are on their way to Puerto Vedra by now. If there's any trouble, they were delivered to the airport by a girl who works for me. And to make doubly certain, they were in an envelope with my business address on it. Why do you have to do this to me, Dougal?"

Macneil fished in the pocket of his jeans. He pulled a squashed cigarette from the pack and rolled it straight.

"I thought you'd get a laugh out of it. All those security precautions and me going smack through the middle like the Invisible Man. And I'll tell you something. A helicopter landed on the back stretch while I was there. I want to bet that's what all the fuss was about."

Fletcher almost choked. "Don't tell me what you think. I don't want to hear about it. All it needs is one little whisper and I'm through. I'm sixty-four years old with a duodenal on the point of bursting. Anywhere else in the world I'm on the garbage heap. If P.I.D.E. hears about this it means my license gone — everything." He drew his finger across his throat in a tragic gesture.

"You're breaking my heart." Macneil put some coins on the table. "Who's *going* to whisper to P.I.D.E. for crissakes? I tell you, they never even looked at my camera."

Fletcher shook his head. "Wise guy. Wait till you're hanging upside down in some cellar, water coming out of your ears and nose."

"Boy, you really *are* conditioned," said Macneil. "If that's what it does to you . . ."

"That's *exactly* what it does to you," Fletcher said heavily. "You do me a favor, Dougal. Forget me for about three months, will you?" He pulled his shabby hat over his ears and stood up.

Macneil raised a hand in farewell. "I'm sorry, Charley. I guess I shouldn't have said anything. I'll be waiting for the light in the window."

He watched Fletcher hurry away, tall and angular. All it needed was a puff of smoke, he thought sourly. Vanished — one elderly American, scared and unfriendly. He should have remembered the old boy's phobia. People talked about "Charley's P.I.D.E. hang-up," but always behind his back. The facts beyond that were never discussed.

He was halfway home when he detected a rattle in the front end of the Volkswagen. He pulled to the side and left the wheel. The noise came from a loose fender rod. It was past one by the church clock when he rounded the square. He parked outside the faded gas pump. A board hung on it said:

HOY   NO   HAY

It had hung there for three years — ever since the new chain of filling stations had put Juanito out of business. He'd gone right back to his father's trade, mending cart-axles. The old man was sitting in the shade of the pump, a fighting cock held between his knees. He was honing a tiny pair of spurs. Macneil proffered the battered pack of butts. The bird would fight in the cool of the evening, in a

39

flurry of steel and feathers. Only one cock left each contest alive. The old man shifted his blanket. He chose a cigarette from the pack with the utmost care, made the token gesture of refusal and tucked it behind his ear.

Macneil pointed into the dark interior of the building behind. "Is Juanito in?"

The old man looked up at him blankly. Macneil touched flame to his own cigarette and put his feet on the spent match. Somebody closed the garage door from the inside. He bent a little lower, remembering the old man's deafness.

"I'll leave the car here," he bawled. "Tell your son I'll see him after the siesta."

He sensed rather than saw the movement and turned swiftly. He was just in time to see Juanito's face disappear from the window. He shrugged and walked away. The art of living with these people was to accept their idiosyncracies. He crossed the square and turned the corner. There was no one on the street but Tia Ana. As he came near his own house, she moved like a marionette, lifting and lowering her arm jerkily. Her seamed face turned toward him. He could see her lips moving but heard nothing. A one-eared cat streaked from under her skirts and clawed its way up a nearby wall. He stood for a second watching the crone. If it hadn't been for the cat, he would have blamed his imagination. Tia Ana was quite still again, her hands gripping her knees, her head bent.

He pushed the patio door. The gate behind was open. Pilar was standing on the far side of the patio, holding her stomach as if she were about to vomit. The maid poised behind her, like a mongoose preparing to strike. A man stepped from behind the door, kicking it shut. The gun he was holding was trained on Macneil's chest. The Canadian backed up hastily.

"What in hell's going on here — who are you?"

The stranger was well over six feet. A bristle of iron-gray hair topped hard black eyes, a strong stern face. His Spanish was fluent but heavily accented.

"Empty your pockets onto the table. Use your hands one at a time and slowly."

Macneil looked across at his wife, dumbfounded. She was desperately pale beneath her tan. Her voice was close to hysteria.

"For God's sake do as he says, darling!"

A magazine lay open on the table by the hammock. A glass of milk beside a half-eaten sandwich. Pilar had obviously been lying there. He emptied his pockets, displaying the meager haul. The crumpled pack of cigarettes, a few bills and coins. His hands had started to tremble.

The stranger came close enough for Macneil to smell the mixed fragrance of cologne and cigar leaf. There was blood on the man's collar. He felt beneath the Canadian's armpits and explored his waistline. He dropped the gun in his jacket pocket with a casual gesture.

"Let me introduce myself. Colonel Weber, P.I.D.E." His face was even bleaker when he smiled.

The door to Macneil's room was open. A quick glance showed that the shelves of the cupboard had been ransacked. There was a canvas bag on the floor, crammed with photographic material. Envelopes full of negatives;

unused film packs; his Rolleiflex camera. He stared at it with disbelief. Pilar was crying silently. Her eyes implored him for caution. The maid was still standing close to her.

Suddenly it was all very clear. The scene at the garage, the crone on the street outside. News of police in the village would run like fire behind locked doors and shut windows. Each had tried to warn him in his own way. His mouth was very dry. He wet it cautiously.

"Don't I have the right to ask what this is about?"

Weber bent and zipped up the canvas bag. He looked at Macneil for fully a minute before answering.

"Let me give you some advice, Señor Macneil. Stop talking about your rights."

He wheeled as the maid broke from behind Pilar. She ran forward, fingers crooked like talons, spitting a phrase in the harsh Indian language. The colonel backhanded her neatly. The blow sent her staggering. She collapsed on the floor, covering her mouth and whimpering.

Macneil caught his wife in his arms. He held her shaking body tight, speaking over her shoulder.

"Are you out of your mind! Can't you see you've got a pregnant woman on your hands?"

Weber picked up the bag again. His face was completely expressionless.

"You can bring your cigarettes. You won't need your money."

Macneil stayed where he was, holding his wife by the shoulders. She slipped from his grasp, mascara streaking her cheeks.

"I think you know the name Gregório Paláu, Colonel Weber. In case you don't, he's a Supreme Court lawyer. He's also a family friend. The moment you take my husband from this house I intend to telephone him."

Weber shepherded Macneil to the door. "You'll be very foolish, senőra. Your husband and I can settle this between us, I hope. But do as you wish."

Her eyes sought her husband. He spoke in English. "Tell him I think it's to do with this morning — up on the racetrack." Weber hustled him out to the street.

Tia Ana had vanished. A signal seemed to have emptied the square. Only a few dogs lay there, slack-jawed in the heat. The police launch Macneil had seen earlier was bobbing against the truck tires roped to the seawall. A uniformed cop was in the control cabin. Another castoff. The launch leaped forward. The Canadian grabbed at the rail. Gulls swooped overhead, raucous in pursuit.

The helmsman headed the launch at the city across the bay. Macneil wiped the spray away mechanically. His mind was completely dulled. Resentment hardened as he remembered the look on his wife's face. The launch came around in a wide arc finishing in front of the police quay. A white jeep was waiting there for them. Macneil climbed into the back with Weber. They raced uptown, siren shrieking, skidding on the streetcar tracks as they climbed the hill. They stopped in a small square near the university. A high wall surrounded cloistered buildings. Gates opened and closed behind them. Macneil waited for the colonel's signal to descend. Weber jerked his head. Everything was quiet and peaceful. Doves strutted

43

across the grass. Water splashed in a basin. Over on the right was what looked like a guardhouse. The colonel's eyes flickered but Macneil had seen enough in the brief second. This man was his enemy.

He walked down a passage, alone with the colonel. The men from the jeep had gone into the guardhouse. Weber opened a door at the end of the passage. The clicking of typewriters came from the next room. Weber seated himself behind the desk. He spoke with contemptuous assurance.

"Shut the door, please."

He started unpacking the bag he had brought, placing the contents in neat order. He inspected each item minutely, matching negatives to prints, checking the seals on unused film packs. He removed the back of the camera and stared through the lens. Macneil was still standing. It was a quarter-hour before Weber raised his head. He considered Macneil for a while, grunted and repacked the bag. He took off his jacket, putting his gun on the blotter in front of him.

"You know why you're here, of course."

Macneil's answer was equally blunt. "Not until you tell me, no."

Weber leaned well back, lighting a thin black cheroot. Each movement was unhurried. His eyes never left Macneil's face.

"In that case, we'll have to help you. We mustn't keep you in suspense. You've been brought here because you were in a prohibited area with a camera this morning."

The irony was blatant but Macneil kept his temper. "In the first place I had no idea that the hippodrome was a prohibited area. In the second place, I had a perfectly good reason for being there. I went up to take some shots of the city. I'm doing an article for a magazine — the pictures are to illustrate it. I've already explained all this to your men."

"But not to me." Weber passed his hand over cropped gray hair and inspected his palm curiously. "What happened to the films you took?"

Macneil blinked, remembering Fletcher. The wrong move now and they'd have Charley in here so fast that his feet wouldn't touch the ground. They'd strip him of his license, probably jail him. He did his best with a frank smile.

"It's a pity the officers didn't ask me at the time. It would have saved a lot of trouble. You see, my trip up there was a dead loss. My assignment calls for color. When I got up to the hippodrome I found that the only film I'd taken was black and white."

Smoke drifted in front of Weber's eyes. "Very odd. I put the same question to your wife. She seems to think that you *did* take pictures."

An ice-cold hand laid fingers on Macneil's spine. He did his best to remember if he'd told Pilar where he was taking the film. All he'd said was the city — he was sure of it.

He moved his feet. "This is kind of embarrassing for me. I don't know if you've had the experience of pregnant women. They're not the easiest people in the world to get along with. My wife knew where I'd gone and why. I've got a reputation for forgetfulness. I told a lie rather than have any argument."

Weber's expression was noncommittal. He opened a

buff folder. "Dougal Macneil, born Vancouver, British Columbia, fourteenth of August, nineteen thirty. You landed here from Puerto Vedra on the tenth of December, nineteen sixty-one. You described yourself then on the entry form as a 'field prospector' employed by the Nippigon Wolfram Company. What exactly does that mean — 'field prospector'?"

Macneil shifted a shoulder. Every foreigner had a dossier. It was disturbing to see it sitting next to a loaded Luger.

"It can mean practically anything, I guess. With Nippigon it was a kind of roving commission. You know — finding contacts — keeping your ear to the ground. There was a percentage on any completed business."

The sweat patches were growing under Weber's arms. He turned the pages of Macneil's passport.

"You're a widely traveled man. Chile — Bolivia — Tripoli — Israel. Is there wolfram in Israel?"

Macneil felt as if something was showing on his face that shouldn't be there. "There's no wolfram in Eire either but I've been there. I wasn't always working, remember. I'd water-ski — that sort of thing. Israel was part of a cruise."

Weber offered his bleak smile. "Then you returned to South America. What brought you to Montoro — business or pleasure?"

The way it was said reminded Macneil of another voice. His father's as he looked up from his rose bushes. *In a country that's lousy with mining engineers, you've got a chance in a million — take it!* The sequel had been entry into a world of desperate endeavor and useless journeys.

A world where a man's given word was the signal for the understanding wink. Weber's question was simple enough to answer. He'd landed in Ciudad de Montoro in the height of summer. A marimba band playing under his hotel balcony had drawn him out to the street. It was another existence entirely. He'd stood there, drinking in the sweet striking smell of the *dama-de-noche* trees. It was past midnight but children were everywhere. People passed him, laughing and chattering. A taco-stand vendor offered cylinders of maize meal stuffed with hot meat sauce. He'd bought one and joined the strollers, aware of dark-eyed girls whose every step was a challenge to their virginity. And suddenly he'd known he was home. He'd gone back up to his room feeling that he'd shed a ton of chains. Ten minutes later, he'd written his letter of resignation.

He tried to put it into words for Weber's benefit. "This'll probably sound fanciful but if Montoro had been a woman, I'd have fallen in love with her. As it was, I did the next best thing. I married a Montoresa."

Weber closed the dossier. His manner changed abruptly. There was a hint of viciousness in the way his mouth snapped shut.

"You're a long way from being a fool, Macneil. And you've been around. You know what the next move is."

Macneil raised his head slowly. The doves were on the grass outside, preening themselves in the sunshine. The typewriters clattered away in the next room. He knew in the pit of his stomach that Weber would no longer accept the truth. It was too late for it.

"You're talking in riddles," he said.

Weber was already on his feet, leaning hard on a button. The door burst open. A couple of tough-looking plainclothesmen ranged themselves alongside Macneil. He found himself being marched out of the office, down the cloistered corridor and across the courtyard. For one wild second he thought they were going to shoot him. Neither man spoke. One of them wore a Christian Action button in his lapel. They walked under an arch into a small cobbled yard. What had once been stables had been converted into garages and a cellblock. One of the men undid a heavy door. A quick thrust sent Macneil staggering into the darkness inside. It was sometime before his eyes adjusted to the obscurity. What light there was came from barred windows high above his head. There was no furniture in the large cell. No utensils or drinking water. He spun around, sensing movement behind him. A blur of white showed against the wall.

"Who is it?" There was no answer.

He walked forward, peering. The vague shape materialized into a man leaning against the wall, watching him. There was ample light to make out a head of reddish hair, a fleshy nose hooked over a mobile mouth. The man was in his early thirties and dressed in a white linen suit. Macneil fished the pack of cigarettes from his pocket. It was still half-full.

"*Habla Español?*" he asked tentatively. He went through the motions of striking a light. "Matches?" he tried in English.

There was no response. He dropped the cigarettes back in his shirt pocket.

"Jesus, *God!*" he said with feeling. It was a relief to talk — even to himself. He started to pace the cell. Fifteen steps — turn — fifteen back to the door. The stranger watched him impassively. Half an hour went by. A stream of water hit the window overhead. Someone was using a hose outside. A cracked voice started singing, the song punctuated with much clearing of the throat. A second voice bawled across the yard.

"Olá — Carlitos!"

The water drowned out the answer. The second voice sounded again, loud and bantering. Macneil stopped dead in his tracks. He spoke in English intuitively.

"Did you hear what those jokers just said — we're going to have a visit." The nervous laugh died in his throat.

The redheaded man was near the door, beckoning Macneil to come closer. He took the Canadian's arm warningly, tracing the letter *L* on the whitewashed wall. He glanced sideways, his eyes questioning. Macneil nodded. The finger traced the message, one letter after another.

l-i-s-t-e-n-i-n-g

He pointed at the ceiling, put his palms against his ear and described a squiggle of wire in the air. His voice came as a shock, loud and with an American accent.

"I don't know what these guys think they're up to — I've been here since eight o'clock this morning. What is it, a revolution?"

Macneil eyed him cautiously. If they were talking for the record, he had problems of his own. He wasn't too sure about the guy anyway. The miming bit was a little too much. He could well be a plant.

Footsteps outside took him off the hook. The door was thrown open. Weber came in followed by the two men who had escorted Macneil to the cell. Weber was without jacket and tie. The Luger was tucked into his waistband. One of the plainclothesmen set two trestles in the middle of the room, three feet apart. The other unfastened the leather case he was carrying. In it was a small generator with a crank. Weber nodded. The redheaded man's lunge came too late. The cops trapped him in a shoulder lock. They laid him face down, one trestle supporting his chest, the other his belly. Their joint weight pinned his head and buttocks.

Weber ripped the man's trousers and underpants down to his ankles. He taped a couple of electrodes to the man's genitals and started cranking the generator. The man's body stiffened. Weber cranked faster, his face tense with effort. The man jerked convulsively like a decapitated hen. He screamed just once and was silent. The colonel wrenched the electrodes free and wiped his fingers fastidiously. The plainclothesmen dragged the stranger across the floor to the wall. They repacked the generator and carried the trestles out into the blinding sunshine. From beginning to end not one word of command had been spoken.

Macneil's hands were clammy and shaking. He watched with sick fascination as the colonel came forward, smiling. Weber's invitation was almost polite.

"Shall we go back to my office? I believe you have something to say to me."

Macneil followed in a daze. He could hear children's

50

voices beyond the high wall. Doves waddled away over the grass. It was senseless, brutal and terrifyingly real. Weber shut the door behind them with his foot. It was twenty past five by the clock on the wall and still no sign of Paláu. Pilar must have been able to reach him by now. Weber pulled a chair for Macneil to sit on. He indicated the plate of sandwiches on the desk. There was a bottle of beer and a glass.

"Go ahead and eat. You must be hungry."

Macneil obeyed automatically. The food was tasteless but he'd eaten nothing since the fish with Fletcher. He drained the beer at a gulp. There were matches on the desk. He lit a cigarette with fingers that were still shaking.

Weber sat down opposite. He locked his hands behind his head. "You're not a Jew," he challenged. "Why do you do their work?"

Macneil coughed on the strong salt burn. "I don't know what you mean."

"You know," smiled Weber, "I'm German but I'm neither for Jews nor against them. My job's to prevent subversive activity of any kind. There's neither room nor reason for Jewish activities in this country."

Macneil crossed his legs. The answering smile — a couple of intelligent men settling a misunderstanding.

"You're not suggesting surely that I've got something to do with espionage? *Jewish* activities? You've got to be joking, Colonel."

Weber tilted his chair back. "You've got a lot at stake, Macneil. How about your wife — do you think your Jewish friends will worry about her?"

51

It was more than Macneil could take. Weber had wrapped films and Jews together and thrown him in for good measure. He leaned forward, emphasizing his words.

"I think you mean all this. In some incomprehensible way I really think you mean it! Why don't you just tell me what I'm accused of?"

Weber's fingers massaged his chin. "Very well," he said at last. "You're a Jewish agent acting against the interests of this country. Your only chance is to surrender the films you took this morning. Do that and I'll see you get protection."

Macneil looked at him hopelessly. His only chance lay with Paláu not Weber. Only the lawyer could see clear in this nightmare.

"I ought to be able to laugh," he said. "But I can't. I've been accused of many things in my life. This tops everything."

"*Ja, ja,*" Weber said wearily. "Listen to me, Macneil. I'm not asking for names. I don't expect you to know them. All I want is the films."

They stared at one another in silence. Weber shrugged, looking up at the clock.

"You will speak, of course," he promised. "Before the night's out you'll speak."

He touched the bell. The same two men were waiting outside.

"Put him back," said Weber. He went out ahead of them, long legs striding down the corridor. There was no sign of him by the time Macneil and his escort reached the entrance courtyard. Long shadows slanted over the cobbles outside the cell. A half-raised shutter opposite offered a glimpse of a water-cannon truck. The heavy door opened and shut leaving Macneil on the inside. He stood quite still, getting his bearings. The Jew lay in a heap on the floor. Macneil bent over him. Hands gripped him by the shirt with unexpected force, pulling him down. The Jew's mouth was close to the Canadian's ear.

"Don't talk any louder than this. Where's Weber?"

The smell of the man's sweat was feral. His recovery was staggering.

"He's gone," breathed Macneil. "I don't know where but he said he'd be back."

The Jew made a funnel with his hands. "He'll be back. Do you want to stay alive?" His knees pinned Macneil against the wall suddenly. "Do you want to stay alive?" he repeated. Something beyond words passed between them — a reminder of savagery that shocked Macneil to silence.

"I mean it," the Jew whispered. "I *know* this guy."

Macneil's brain refuted the implication. "They wouldn't dare. I've got a wife here — friends."

"I don't care *what* you've got," the Jew whispered savagely. "Neither of us is going to leave here alive unless we help one another."

The picture was suddenly clear — implacable eyes above a smiling mouth. Acceptance bludgeoned its way into his head. The Jew was telling the truth. Incredible or not, Weber intended to kill them. Sweat trickled down through Macneil's hair. His voice was barely audible.

"We've got no chance. This is P.I.D.E. headquarters. There are cops all over the place."

The Jew rocked him by the shoulder. "How far are we from that guardroom at the front?"

"A hundred and fifty yards. A little more, maybe."

The Jew pulled off his right shoe. He held it by the upper and tugged hard at the heel. A band of adhesive snapped. The bottom half of the heel slid forward, revealing a hollow space the size of a matchbox. The Jew used his nail to prise out what looked like a tiny cigarette lighter. It was wrapped in a sheaf of thousand peso notes. The heel clicked back. The Jew put his shoe back on. He leaned forward so that his face was close to Macneil's ear again.

The Canadian hauled himself up. He crossed the cell to the door and looked back. The redheaded man nodded. Macneil's thumb found the bell push. He stood there, his heart banging in his rib cage, thinking of what came next. Seconds crept by. The Jew lay sprawled on the ground, trousers around his ankles, as Weber had left him. Macneil pushed the bell again, stabbing it like a man in despair. He put his ear to the crack in the door. There was the sound of running footsteps — a man's voice outside — irate and out of breath.

"What's the trouble in there?"

"Get me out of here!" yelled Macneil. He beat on the door with both fists. "This guy's not breathing anymore. I want to see the colonel!"

He heard the two men muttering, then a key invaded the lock. The door swung wide. It was the same two plain-

clothesmen as before. Both carried guns in their hands.
The one with the curly black hair blocked the doorway.
He peered past Macneil suspiciously. The Canadian
stepped back. The whitewashed walls were filthy in the
light from the yard. Rusty stains showed at about the
height of a man's head. He pointed at the huddle of
clothes.

"I want out of here. He's dead."

"Watch him, Paco!" the curly-headed man pushed by.
His companion moved to Macneil's side. The Jew's hand
flashed as the cop bent over him, discharging the ammonia
spray. The cop staggered back, clawing at his eyes. The
other came at Macneil. The Canadian ducked sideways.
The butt of the gun came down hard, glancing off his
shoulder. He kicked out at his assailant's groin. The
plainclothesman gasped with agony. He pitched forward
slowly. His head hit the concrete. The noise was like a
butcher's cleaver hitting the block. Blood gushed from
his nose and mouth. Macneil stumbled away, sickened.
The whole cell reeked of the ammonia that stung his eyes.
The Jew grabbed the gun from the floor and thumbed the
safety catch up. Macneil faced him across two prostrate
bodies. The pool of blood was the size of a football. A
nerve started to jump near Macneil's right eye. It was
hard not to voice his secret fear.

"We can't leave him like this."

The Jew's mouth twisted. "I can. Come on — let's get
out of here." They inched out into the bright evening sunshine. There was no one in sight. The Jew locked the cell
door and dropped the key through a grating. The outer

wall was directly behind the makeshift cellblock. It was twenty feet high. The Jew ducked under the garage shutters. He was out again almost immediately, beckoning to Macneil. The Canadian went in after him. A ladder was hooked on the wall. He shook his head.

"It won't reach."

The Jew paid no attention. He unhooked the ladder. "Take the other end."

They ran it across the yard and propped it against the boundary wall. The highest rung was a good ten feet from the top. The gun barrel had raised a hard lump on Macneil's shoulder. He rubbed it painfully. Only part of his brain seemed to be working. The rest was numbed by the sound of a head crashing against concrete. He was perversely ready to lose and at the same time blame the other for losing.

The Jew wedged the ladder with a piece of wood. He took his jacket off and gave it to Macneil.

"You go first. I'll lift you by the ankles. There's wire on top. Spread the coat over it. Lean in, keep your hands flat against the wall and don't look down."

Macneil kicked out of his sandals. He stuffed them into his hip pockets and started up the ladder. His back felt very vulnerable. He was well above the roofline, a perfect target for a rifle poked through a guardroom window. The Jew was right behind him. The ladder sagged under their joint weight. Macneil could go no farther. He looked up between outstretched arms. His fingertips were still a couple of feet from the top of the wall. He felt his ankles grasped then the shudder in the Jew's muscles as he lifted his burden. Macneil's palms scraped up over the stone-work. The gap grew narrower. The Jew's arms were shaking dangerously. Macneil clutched desperately, hooking the jacket on the wire and finding a handhold. He chinned himself and rolled sideways. Barbs nicked his buttocks. He straddled the wall, gripping the wire with his left hand, offering his right to the Jew. He pulled himself erect, flesh and lungs protesting. Then the Jew was there beside him. They swung out together, hitting the ground simultaneously. The Jew's jacket still hung on the wire.

The deserted street formed the third side of a square that enclosed the palace. The houses opposite were silent and shuttered. It was a wealthy neighborhood and summertime. The owners would be in the mountains. A dog rose from the dust at the bottom of a tree. It took a couple of stiff-legged paces toward them, barked once and urinated. It lay down again, watching them as they ran for the back of the square. Macneil's bare feet thudded on the sidewalk. The Jew was running easily, his elbows pressed against his ribs, his knees coming up in a high pumping action. A quarter-mile away, they eased to a walk. Macneil leaned against a tree, fighting for breath. There was no sound of pursuit — nothing but the rasping of cicadas in the walled gardens facing them.

The Jew mopped his face. He pushed the Luger out of sight beneath his shirt. The once white trousers were filthy.

"Where the hell are we — we've got to keep moving."

They had stopped a hundred yards from the small park on the crest of the hill.

"San Vincente," said Macneil. He pointed ahead. "If we cut through the park and out the other side we're in the Old City."

They started to walk again. The Jew's eyes were everywhere. "The minuet's over," he said. "You didn't do that guy's head any good. They'll shoot first and ask the questions afterward."

The words seemed to staple them together, the implication deadly.

"It was an accident," Macneil muttered. Just saying it was a relief.

The Jew was combing his hair as he went. He licked his palm and smoothed a stubborn plume at the back.

"Try telling that to Weber!"

Macneil grabbed his arm and swung him around. "You *wanted* it to happen, you bastard! You wanted me on the run!"

The redheaded man shook himself free. "Take your goddam hands off me, you clown! Can't you see our only chance is to stick together?"

They walked through the gates into the park. Shrill-voiced children were playing under the watchful eyes of nursemaids. An old man was sitting in the fading sunshine, dozing with the stillness of death. A white cane lay across his lap. The alms box beside him was fastened to his wrist with a length of lavatory chain. Macaws screamed in the hibiscus trees as the two men hurried underneath. They stopped behind a statue of Bolívar. The road beyond the railings dropped sharply. Behind the stepped roofs of the Old City was the bay. Almirón was a white cluster of buildings tinged red by the setting sun.

The Jew winced, bending double as he clutched his groin. His face was covered with sweat when he straightened up.

"I'll be all right," he said. "Another half-hour and it'll be dark. Are you coming with me or not?"

Macneil looked at him impassively. A sense of rage and frustration had replaced his fear. It colored his acceptance of loneliness — the certainty that the Jew had used him. He was *still* being used. The Jew spoke no Spanish. He didn't even know where he was.

"I don't have an alternative," Macneil said quietly. "But I'll have to get a message to my wife first."

The Jew shook his head. "You're crazy, man. Weber will have a stakeout on every house you ever visited. The phones'll be tapped. Look — I *know* this score. Wait until we get to Puerto Vedra."

"*Puerto Vedra?*" Macneil exploded. The throwaway line only accentuated the lunacy of their position. "You're the one who's crazy. You talk as if the frontier's a couple of blocks away. It's seventeen miles."

The Jew was actually smiling. He put his finger to his head and pulled an imaginary trigger.

"That's what we get if we hang around here. We'd better start moving."

They walked down the hill, keeping in the growing shadow. The Jew investigated each corner with the delicacy of a hunted fox. The flutter of his fingers either encouraged or restrained Macneil who followed like a sleepwalker. They were already deep into the Old City, a neighborhood of third-rate hotels, seamen's bars and cheap stores. Street stands were jammed against the sidewalks. The surrounding air hung in a blue pall, reeking of oil-fried fish. Evening shoppers jostled whores smiling from the doorways. The traffic crawled to an accompaniment of klaxons sounding. The two men were swallowed in the tumult like gnats in an anthill.

Macneil shouldered his way through the crowd, keeping a couple of yards behind his companion. A dirty white cap, grabbed from God knows where, covered the Jew's flaming hair. He seemed to have grown at once shorter and older, limping along with hunched back. The street came to an abrupt end. Sodium lamps hung above the embarcadero. Water slapping against the seawall mirrored their light. Darkness had come with the suddenness of the tropics. The port terminal blazed a half-mile away. The boat for Puerto Vedra was brilliantly white in the arcs suspended above her moorings. A network of crane booms showed against the purple night. They were sheltering in a ship chandler's doorway. The Jew glanced across the concourse. A double line of cars was parked around the bullring.

"Does anyone watch those cars?"

It was almost ten o'clock. The old bullfighter would have been wheeled home by now.

Macneil shrugged. "He's gone. Why?"

The Jew smiled again. "We're going to borrow one."

"You're out of your mind," said Macneil. "These people may be short on highway patrols but they've got a good solid line in roadblocks. Besides, they'd have the numbers on the air before we were out of the city."

The Jew pulled his cap over his eyes. His confidence seemed complete.

"We're going to make sure they do. You cover me. If anyone comes near, whistle. Just do like this." He pursed his lips. The notes were low and surprisingly sweet — like a boy calling his sweetheart.

There were thirteen cars. Macneil counted them super-stitiously, standing where the Jew had stationed him, his back flat against the warm red brick. His skin crawled in sympathy as the Jew walked forward. He peered after him anxiously. Footsteps on the far side of the bullring echoed inside the empty stadium. It was difficult to place them precisely. He could just see the Jew's head in that crazy cap. The guy wasn't even making an attempt to conceal himself. Trying the goddam doors as if he had a license. Suddenly the Jew vanished. Macneil glimpsed him in the front seat of a red convertible. The Canadian moved left, whistling frantically. Someone was crossing the concourse. The newcomer was on them in seconds. He opened up a small panel truck. The headlamps came on, catching Macneil against the wall in full glare. He stood perfectly still, his eyes shut tight, denying the whole thing.

The truck backed up, wheeled and then shot off along the embarcadero. Macneil wiped his palms on his jeans. What the hell was the guy *doing*. The Jew was out of the convertible, bending down at the rear. He used a wrench to unfasten the license plates then did the same at the

61

front. He walked over to the neighboring car and switched the two sets of identification. Only then did he come to Macneil — an easy stroll that ended a foot away from the Canadian's hiding place.

Macneil looked at him defensively. "What's the matter with you — what are you staring at?"

The Jew pushed his cap back. The moon was just rising. There was enough light to see the irony in his face.

"Do you always panic like that? That guy couldn't see me."

Macneil's answer was hot with anger. "What do you think I am — some sort of cheap hoodlum who's used to this kind of thing? I didn't even know where he came from. For all I knew he might have crawled in there right beside you."

The Jew's hands pantomimed apology. "Forget it. You saw me switch those plates. That means that if the car *is* missed, it won't be us they're looking for."

Macneil nodded, understanding. It made sense. Few people knew the numbers on their license plates. Fewer still checked them at ten o'clock at night. One thought led to another.

"Don't tell me the guy left his keys for you."

The Jew took his arm, leading him to the red Mustang. The white upholstery smelled of a woman. A pair of doeskin gloves was draped over the steering column. The Jew put the Luger in the lift-up compartment between them. He bent under the dash and yanked out a fistful of wires. He seemed to know exactly what he was doing. He selected two wires and spliced them together. The eight

cylinders fired immediately. The motor settled to a steady
hum. The Jew pulled his door shut. There was a hint of
mockery in his voice.

"More hoodlum stuff, I'm afraid. I'm sorry about it.
Better fasten your seat belt."

Macneil buckled the webbing without a word. The redheaded man appeared to read his mind.

"If there's a roadblock we go straight through it." He
was staring out over the seawall. The night boat was a
mile away, decks ablaze with lights and heading north.
He nodded as if to himself. "With any luck we'll be there
before her. That's all we need, a little luck."

There were cigarettes and matches in the glove compartment. Macneil lit a butt. It seemed that the decisions
weren't his to make. All he had to do was accept them. It
was hardly in character.

"Sure." He said it as lightly as he could. "Sure, that's all
we need, a little luck."

The Jew shifted into gear. "You're the pilot. How do
we go?"

Macneil hunched his knees. "Straight along the embarcadero. You'll see a loop-road posted a couple of miles on.
It'll bring you onto the marginal highway, well out of the
city."

The Jew touched the gas pedal. He brought the Mustang up to fifty and held it there. The streetlights flicked
by. He switched on the radio. Neither man spoke. Macneil's thoughts were with Pilar. Paláu would have to bring
her out of Montoro. No matter what happened, there was
no longer any future for them here. He had no idea where

they would go. All the doctors had said that a first baby needed expert attention. Canada? The thought filled him with misgiving. He imagined the country, still in the grip of winter — the house on Burrard Inlet, disturbed by a baby's bawling. Worst of all was the picture of his father, restless in the company of a daughter-in-law he didn't know and must fail to understand. That faint hope fell like a stone. He'd been away too long, for crissakes. An Anglo-Saxon world would stifle them both.

He lowered the window letting the breeze bathe his hot face. A sign came up ahead.

LA FRONTERA Y PUERTO VEDRA   33 KILOMETROS

"Easy does it," he advised. "There's sand on the road now."

If the driver heard he showed no sign of it. He was whistling through his teeth. The Demon Driver, Macneil thought morosely. He should have insisted on taking the wheel. Insist? Well . . .

Lights twinkled on the hills to their left. The Jew swung the car wide, hitting the marginal highway at eighty miles an hour. He cut his headlamps. The bright moon etched the pattern of beach and palm trees. The roar of the surf was loud. The wide tires hissed over the film of sand. Macneil pitched his butt through the window. The way the guy was driving they'd be lucky to make the ten kilometer post. It was one way out.

"A few more miles." His chin was between his knees, his feet up on the seat. "Then it all happens. There's a bridge over the Rio Verde — a cutoff to that headland on our right. That's where my lawyer lives. My wife'll be there. If there's going to be a roadblock, that's the place for it."

The Jew suspended his toneless whistling. "If we crash you're on your own. Everyone for himself, understood?"

Macneil put the question he'd been hoarding. *Someone* had to give him the answers.

"You've never asked me what I was doing in P.I.D.E. headquarters. Does that mean you already know?"

A man cut into the samba music with a news flash. A fire in a downtown paper warehouse. No mention of a jail-break. The Jew's eyes were on the road ahead.

"It means I don't *want* to know."

"Not even about the film?" Macneil persisted. "Weber thought you did."

The Jew shook his head. "We'll talk about it. How far now?"

The headland was coming up fast. A thousand acres of savannah-covered bluff jutted out to sea. It formed the northern horn of the bay. Pilar was somewhere there, in the wedding-cake mansion overlooking the estuary.

"Around the next bend," he said. "And you're on the bridge."

He closed his eyes, pushing his feet against the floorboards as the Mustang fought the curve. He heard it scrape the cactus on the shoulder of the highway. The boarding over the bridge rattled. He opened his eyes expecting lights and a barrier, armed men flagging them down. The bridge was empty. The rapids boiled below, cascading to calmer waters and the distant estuary. They rolled off onto the highway. The Jew brought the Mustang to a halt. He reached across and took one of the cigarettes. He held it the way a nonsmoker does, like a pencil.

"Well *say* something!" he challenged. "Smile!"

Macneil pulled his legs up again. The guy was human after all. His hand was actually shaking.

"It was the obvious place," the Canadian said. "There's nothing now till we reach the frontier. We can't take the car much farther. We'll have to ditch it."

The Jew pulled the sheaf of thousand-peso bills from his pocket. He peeled off two and tucked them into Macneil's shirt. His smile grew more saturnine by the minute.

"Three blind mice — Weber, you and me. Are you going to take me across the frontier, friend?"

Macneil stared out in front of him. There was nothing now between them and the customs post. The breeze carried the musty stink of the jungle swamps. He knew the creeks from Paláu's alligator hunts. The mosquito coast was uninhabited. It was also impassable on foot. The Guardia Nacional manned the area. They operated in teams of two, each team responsible for its own territory. They lurked behind driftwood shelters on the beaches, vigiled in the mangrove swamps. He'd stumbled on them sometimes, walking around the bay in the evening, their cigarettes glowing in the twilight.

He unbuckled his seat belt. "Where else is left to go?"

The Jew took the Luger out and stuffed it in his belt. "Funny. We don't even know one another's names."

Macneil wanted to laugh in his face. What the hell did names matter. He controlled his voice. He was getting jumpy and he needed his cool.

"We could call one another Smith." The other man

nodded, still smiling. There was a shopping pad with a pencil attached in the glove compartment. Macneil drew a rough map.

"This is the highway. It forks west to the customs post. That's three miles away. We've got to take a straight line across *here*, on foot."

"That means leaving the car. It'll have to be out of sight."

Macneil used the pencil again.

He put his finger inside the triangle. "What isn't swamp is jungle. There's supposed to be this trail across it." He sketched the beginning of a line.

The Jew looked up doubtfully. "*Supposed* to be?"

The Canadian crumpled the piece of paper and flicked it through the window.

"I know where it starts. The Indians claim that it comes out near Chiclana. That's in Puerto Vedra."

"We'll take it," the Jew decided. "And the car?"

Macneil nodded ahead. "Keep going. You're right. We've got to move it off the highway. Trucks come through at this time of night. An abandoned car out here would be reported."

They drove on for a couple of miles. "Hold it!" Macneil pointed down a track on their left. "Down there."

The Mustang rolled over the shoulder and bumped down into a patch of dogwood. Bush scraped along the paintwork. Sharp branches tore into the soft top. Finally the wheels lost traction, spinning uselessly in the soft dark earth. The motor stalled. They forced the doors open and stood looking at one another over the car. Their roles had been reversed. It was the Jew now who was waiting for the lead. They walked back to the highway. The frontier post was no more than a quarter-mile away. A collection of whitewashed shacks, flags and a barrier. An articulated truck zigzagged across the road. Powerful arc lamps showed the uniformed men around it.

"Traffic's light," said Macneil. "And they're bored. They make the most of it. Watch it from now. Stay as close as you can."

They slithered down the bank. The highway was laid on a core of rock dumped into the swampland. The strip of asphalt was fifteen feet above their heads. A different world lay below, of giant *cuipo* trees, hung with orchids, majestic in the rising moon. The air was sweet with the smell of decay. Mosquitoes rose in hungry hordes, striking into their bare flesh savagely.

The Jew was slapping at his legs and face frantically. "Put your socks over your trousers," said Macneil. There was nothing he could do with his sandals except remove them.

Apparently solid ground dissolved into stinking mud. The mocking cry of a bird followed their progress through the still trees. There was a distant glimpse of open water. Saltwater creeks filtered into the jungle from the estuary. He'd explored them a dozen times, using Paláu's shallow-draft speedboat. It all seemed so long ago — Pilar at his side — both of them busy with cameras aimed at the caimans on the sandbars. The bright green ropes of tree snakes, somnolent till disturbed then snapping like whip-lashes, a half-ounce of distilled poison on their ends. He was suddenly conscious of bare feet and ankles. The avenue of giant trees narrowed. The ground grew firmer. He could see the lights from the frontier post reflected in the nearer water. He signaled a halt. They lit cigarettes, clouding themselves in smoke against the biting bugs.

"Another half-hour," guessed Macneil. "And we'll be in Chiclana. There'll be transport there."

The Jew held his cigarette awkwardly. "And no trouble? Two men without passports turning up only a mile away from the frontier?"

Macneil shrugged. He was enjoying the change of pace. It was good to be supplying the answers instead of the questions.

"They'll ask about your money, your health and your women. The one thing they'll *never* ask in Puerto Vedra is where you come from. Let's get going."

The trees began to crowd one another, reducing the moonlight to a crisscross of silver and black. The Jew caught Macneil's sleeve, a quick movement that stopped the Canadian.

"I heard something — ahead," he whispered.

Macneil stared in the same direction. The night was full of sound. He heard nothing to disturb him. He plucked his sleeve free, on the point of being sarcastic, when two men appeared through the trees in front of them. They wore the drab gray and peaked caps of the Guardia Nacional. Each carried a submachine gun.

The Jew dropped like a stone, flat on his face, the Luger already out. Macneil lay beside him, nose and mouth buried in sticky creeper. He pinned the Jew's gun hand with his own.

"Keep still! They haven't seen us."

69

The guards strolled forward. One of them called and his partner crossed the trail. They stood at the edge of the water, staring up into the sky.

"A rocket," one said knowledgeably. They moved off, side by side. Their course carried them twenty feet wide of the two prostrate men.

"*Now!*" said Macneil. They rose together and ran. The Jew with his odd high pumping action, elbows neat against his ribs. They covered fifty yards when the two guns opened up behind them. Shells sprayed the branches over the Canadian's head. He saw the Jew stumble, reaching out for unseen hands to hold. He spun sideways as the marksman completed his figure eight. Macneil went down on one knee. The whole jungle was awake, the darkness furtive with movement. He looked over his shoulder. The guards hadn't changed their position. *Reloading,* he thought desperately. The last blast had taken the Jew in the chest. There was little left of it. He must have been dead before hitting the ground. The Luger was inches from his right hand. The Canadian felt in the dead man's pocket quickly. Money was no good to the Jew now. He found the sheaf of bills and picked up the gun. The Jew's left fist was tightly shut. Macneil prised it open. Inside was a piece of paper, balled as if to be thrown away. He sighted the Luger back along the trail and squeezed the trigger. The heavy gun jumped twice in his hand. The shells whined into the darkness. One of the guards bawled at the other.

"Stay where you are. Be careful!"

The shout spurred Macneil to fresh effort. He ran despairingly, head down, his breathing a tortured whistle.

There were no more shouts, nothing but an animal screaming. The sound died across the water. Thorns and suckers tore at his shirt and jeans. The air seemed starved of oxygen. His feet were beyond feeling. Suddenly he was in the open, in a treeless stretch of lush green grass. The lights of Chiclana burned bright at the end of the trail.

He eased to a staggering walk. Mosquitoes were stabbing at his flanks and back. He was too exhausted to take off his shirt. The Jew's death had left him strangely apathetic. It was difficult to think of the bloody heap of flesh as a human being. He smoothed the scrap of paper between his fingers. The typewritten address was legible in the moonlight.

> Señor D.
> Philip Asher
> Florida Hotel
> Ciudad de Montoro

So that was his name, Asher. He was about to throw it away when he realized the paper was a piece torn from an envelope. The address was typed on a small adhesive label. He picked the label off with his nail. Underneath was a second address.

> Benjamin Shashoua
> Calle Real
> Barrio Viejo
> Puerto Vedra

He crumpled it in his hand and threw it as far as he could.

WERNER WEBER

HE DROVE into the courtyard and parked. The journey down from the plateau had taken longer than he expected. The city was hot and listless. He stood for a while watching the darkened buildings. Everything was strangely quiet. He could hear no more than the splashing of the fountain, the doves in the eaves. His nerves tightened a notch. He walked across to the guardroom and pushed open the door.

The four men inside turned in unison, presenting a ring of startled faces. Moreno's was one of them. Weber's voice was heavily sarcastic.

"I'm not interrupting anything, I hope? Which of you happens to be duty officer?"

"Señor Coronel!" A man with troubled eyes started to detach himself from the group.

The colonel's aide hurried past him. "May I speak to you outside?"

Weber moved slowly, sensing the undercurrent of excitement. The door closed. They were alone in the courtyard. Moreno licked his lips. He hurried the words as if they had been rehearsed for too long.

"The prisoners escaped. They half-blinded Peralta.

The other man's in hospital. The doctors are operating now."

Weber's expression betrayed nothing. He moved and thought in an icy discipline. Above all he had to keep calm. Moreno looked as if his own ghost had chased him through the cloisters.

"Have you put out an alarm?"

Moreno's hands signaled nervous dissent. "No, Colonel. That is, only within the department. We know Macneil's crossed the frontier into Puerto Vedra. The Guardia Nacional telephoned a quarter-hour ago. One of their patrols discovered the fugitives, a couple of kilometers east of Frente Rio. On the old Indian trail. The Jew was shot dead. Macneil escaped. The Guardia wanted to know if we had any interest in them. I played it down. They've got what's left of Asher at the frontier post."

Weber's voice was very quiet. "What exactly did you say to the Guardia?"

Moreno balled his shoulders. "I said we'd never even heard of either of them from the descriptions. I thought that would be what you'd want, sir. That's why I kept off the air. As it is, we can always claim to have made a mistake."

Weber beckoned him away from the guardroom door. "You did the right thing. This affair's got to be kept quiet, at least for the present. You'd better see Peralta yourself, the other man, too, as soon as he's conscious. Make sure neither of them talks. In the meantime I want someone who'll do exactly as he's told. Who is there on duty?"

Moreno's eyes flickered. "There's the Pole."

Weber threw his jacket over his shoulder. "Send him to my office. And stay where I can get hold of you."

He was barely in his chair when a rap came on the door. The man who pushed it open had a narrow head with chalk rings around the pupils of his eyes. His clothes were neat but nondescript. His Spanish was even more heavily accented than Weber's.

"Sergeant Kokoscka, Colonel. You sent for me?"

Weber leaned forward on both elbows. Kokoscka had landed in 1956, traveling on an old Nansen Bureau pass. Weber knew his real name as well as the several prisons he had escaped from. He was a good policeman and both men understood one another.

"Do you know where Almirón is?"

The strange, birdlike eyes were intelligent. "On the marginal highway going south, Colonel."

"Exactly," said Weber. "Pick a couple of men, take a jeep and go to fifteen Calle de Roche. You're looking for a woman — a Señora Macneil. If you don't find her at that address, go straight to the Northern Bluff — the house of a lawyer called Paláu. If she's not at her home, that's where she'll be."

Kokoscka asked no questions nor offered any comment. Weber poked a finger at him.

"Don't come back without her, Sergeant. She's pregnant. You're to treat her with consideration and respect but don't allow any outside interference. Arrest anyone who obstructs you. Clear?"

Kokoscka's thumbs lined the seams of his trousers. "Is that all, Colonel?" He saluted and left.

Weber pulled Macneil's file from the drawer. P.I.D.E.

had nothing on Asher and his own information was meager. Von Ostdorf's friends might have more but it was no time to alarm them. The Jew was dead anyway. It was Macneil who mattered. There had to be something that he'd missed in the file — a clue to the Canadian's double life. He pulled out the worn silver case and lit a cheroot. He studied the pages attentively.

Macneil's cover appeared to have been cleverly produced. The story that emerged was that of a man with few interests beyond his wife and home. The confidential report from the Banco Central showed a modest credit over the years. There were no debts, no scandals, no other women. The list of known associates was a short one. The name of Paláu headed it. Gregorio Paláu, advocate of the Supreme Court. A few more foreigners completed the list. All were residents. The last name was vaguely familiar. He blew a cloud of smoke at the ceiling and concentrated. Suddenly he had it. He leaned across and spoke into the box. The door opened. Moreno came in from the adjoining room. There was no one else there.

"Draw the keys to the Aliens Office," said Weber. "Bring me the file on an American called Fletcher. Charles Fletcher."

Moreno was back in five minutes. He put the buff folder in front of Weber, his voice carefully impersonal.

"There's a message from the communications room, sir. They've just had a signal from Panama. General Zuimárraga is returning tomorrow."

Weber's head came up slowly. "Tomorrow? Do they say why? He's not due for another two days."

Moreno's long thin nose sniffed the air cautiously. "All

they say is that he's coming, sir. That and to have an escort at the airport."

Weber leveled his look on the other's face. As he went, so went Moreno. There had never been any secret about it.

"I'm relying on you, Captain," he said with meaning. "I think you know what I mean. Make sure that there's a proper record of the arrests you and I make. 'Held for interrogation' should cover both of them."

Moreno's expression betrayed his concern. "Does that mean that the escape goes in, sir?"

Weber made a small noise of disapproval. "But of course. The full circumstances, just as they happened. The Jew was a Castro agent."

Moreno whistled. "I'd guessed Russian. And the American?"

"Another from Havana," said Weber. "You see the implications. I shall have to make a full report to the general in person." His mind had already shaped his plan — one that would freeze danger to a minimum. There would be no need to tell Von Ostdorf — no panic — above all, no need to alarm the man in the bunker. No one would be informed except Ilidio Zuimárraga, the scourge of Cuba. The colonel's smile switched on and off. The old German saying made sense now as ever. *Steel in the head, hand and heart.*

He smiled blandly. "Have the matron's rooms prepared for occupation. You'll need blankets and sheets, everything a woman will want. And have a doctor's number ready — a gynecologist. Choose one that we know."

The door closed on his aide. Weber dipped into Fletcher's file and refreshed his memory. He added the dossier to Macneil's, locking them both in the drawer. He put his jacket on and went to the window. The lights were already on upstairs in the opposite wing. The matron's rooms hadn't been used for years. It was a self-contained unit and easy to guard.

It was midnight when he parked on a street near the port. The rambling wooden building opposite had an outside staircase that led to a second-story veranda. There were six empty tables in the garden out front. A shabby sign hung in the trees.

BAR EL PIMPI

The noise he could hear came from a frontón court behind the terrace. There was the crack of rebounding balls, the shouts of the gamblers. He tiptoed up the rickety stairs and stood still. The veranda was dim. He edged toward a crack of light. A voice called out in Spanish as he neared the door.

"It's open."

Weber stepped inside. The room stank of burned food. A pot of beans had erupted onto the gas stove. The floor was littered with newspapers. An elderly man in a T-shirt and shorts was lying on the bed under a lithograph of the president. A grizzled frieze of hair framed his sweating scalp. A plastic fan on a table barely stirred the exhausted air. The man struggled up on one hand. The other held a glass of rum and lime juice.

Weber closed the windows. He swept a chair free of

clothing and sat down. The man on the bed cranked corded legs to the floor. His face was belligerent.

"Who the hell are you?"

"I'll ask the questions," Weber said curtly. "What's your name?"

"Fletcher." The man emptied his glass and looked at the floor between his bony knees. The shadow of the fan blade whirled through the room. "P.I.D.E.?" he said after a while.

Weber cataloged the cheap furniture, the curtained alcove with its shower, the sink unit piled with dirty dishes. The place stank of failure.

"You were obviously expecting someone else, Señor Fletcher. I'm sorry if I disappoint you."

The courtesy was false. The truth was, he'd outgrown this sort of clash. The stale approach to the predictable end.

Fletcher smiled weakly. The effect was spoiled because his teeth were in a glass by the sink. He covered his mouth with his hand, self-consciously.

Weber stretched out a leg, kicking over a pile of periodicals. "Your habits haven't changed, I see. Still the same student of current affairs."

Fletcher shifted on the bed. "I read a lot, if that's what you mean. When you get to my age, that's about what pleasure is. A drink, a book and bed."

Weber fixed his eyes on the artery beating in the stringy neck. "That time they had you down at headquarters — how long ago was it — four years? I want you to tell me just what happened."

Fletcher heaved himself up. He padded to the sink and fiddled with his mouth. Teeth gave his protest a ring of injured innocence.

"I'm not likely to forget. A couple of your men came to my office one afternoon. They closed the place up and took me to San Vincente."

Weber shrugged behind the lighted match. "I know all that. I wanted to hear your version of the reasons behind it. You see, I've never had the pleasure of meeting you, Señor Fletcher."

The travel agent looked at him warily. "I don't know — a lot of junk had been coming to my business address. Commie propaganda, mailed out of East Germany. I'd take it in — what else. Some of it I'd read. The editorials were always good for a laugh."

Weber waited till his cheroot was burning properly. "You must have been bewildered. All this stuff arriving. Strange you didn't think it worthwhile reporting the matter to the authorities."

Fletcher blinked anxiously. "I just didn't think. These things happen. Your name gets on a list and before you know it the whole bit snowballs."

Weber brushed a cloud of smoke away. "As indeed it did. What was it you finally received — an invitation to the World Congress of Youth." His tone was sardonic.

Fletcher's grin was even weaker. "Yeah, well. By that time I had a good idea who was responsible. There was this crackpot teacher at the American school here. God knows why but she wanted to light a fire under me. I hardly knew her."

"Middle-aged virgins," Weber said understandingly. "By then she'd gone back to California. A pity. It meant that your story could never be checked out properly."

Fletcher bent down and retrieved his glass. It was empty but he still drank from it.

"But your people knew the truth. They as good as told me so. All this happened four years ago anyway."

"So it did," agreed Weber. His tone was unchanged. "Tell me something about your friendship with a man called Macneil."

The American's eyes wavered. "Macneil? Hell, you couldn't call us friends — no more than acquaintances. You know, we play cards together, a couple of times a month. That's about it. I haven't seen him in weeks."

"You're a liar," snapped Weber. He walked across to the window and drew the curtain back. The frontón game was over. The terrace bar was crowded. He let the curtain fall again, speaking over his shoulder. "Suppose you were expelled from this country, Señor Fletcher, where would you go?"

He turned sharply. Fletcher's face was pasty with shock. "I've never even thought about it, señor. Why would I — my life's an open book."

Weber cut in savagely. "Then you'd better *start* thinking. You're very near the event. Macneil gave you some films this morning. What did you do with them?"

Fletcher's eyes filled with self-pity. "Eighteen years I've been in this country. It's my home."

Weber took the other man's chin between his fingers, forcing Fletcher to look up.

"The films — what did you do with them?"

The travel agent's voice broke. "I swear to God I didn't know."

"*What* didn't you know?" Weber insisted. "That your friend was in a prohibited area with a camera? Don't tell me you don't know that he's a Communist!"

"A Communist!" The American shook his head hopelessly. "I'm going to give it to you straight. I didn't even know that he'd *been* on the racetrack till it was too late. Do you think I'd have put that package on the plane otherwise? He gave me this pitch about a magazine article. He said that color development was better in Puerto Vedra than here. It could be true. I saw no harm in what I did."

The colonel hardened his voice. "Who was the package consigned to?"

Fletcher's Adam's apple rose in his scrawny throat. "One of the stewards took it. The odd favor, señor. I swear to God . . ."

"What was the address?" insisted Weber. "You'd better remember."

The old man was almost in tears. His nerve ends were near breaking.

"Fotos Janes. Calle Larios."

Weber looked for a place to put his cheroot end. There was none. He threw it at the sink in disgust.

"Try to control yourself, man. Do you realize what this means — I could close your business and throw you in jail! Who's going to worry about *you?*"

A drop fell from the end of Fletcher's nose. "I've always done my best . . ."

"Your best?" Weber said contemptuously. He looked

around the room with distaste. "You live like a pig. You're a failure, Fletcher. From any point of view you're a failure. There's nowhere *for* you to go. No one but me to look to. My name is Colonel Weber. Do you think you'll remember it?"

It was as much as Fletcher's mouth could do to shape the words silently. Weber measured him. The juice was out of the man.

"I'm your only hope, remember that. You could say that there's a bond between us now. You won't open your mouth about this visit to anyone, do you understand? And I might just forget why I came here — at least for the present. What happens afterward . . . that depends."

The American's face collapsed in relief. "I won't say anything, Colonel. Anything I can do at any time — I swear to God . . ."

Weber looked out of the doorway. The veranda and the staircase were empty. He looked back briefly.

"You worry too much about God. Worry about Colonel Weber."

He drove back to headquarters. He made a mental note to get the flight steward's name. Fletcher was a definite asset. A number of foreigners used his travel agency. He left the Mercedes outside the entrance gates and walked across the courtyard to the guardroom. The man on duty stiffened. Weber returned his salute.

"Is Kokoscka back yet?"

The guard indicated the jeep behind the fountain. "Half an hour ago, Colonel. Captain Moreno left a message that he's waiting in his office."

Weber cut across the moonlit grass. Even up here the

air was stifling. The skeleton of his plan was gathering flesh. First came Fletcher, then the woman in the building on his right. Last of all came Zuimárraga.

Moreno's peaked face was sweating under the light from his desk lamp. There was a plate in front of him. He came to his feet hurriedly, wiping his mouth.

"Señora Macneil is here, Colonel. Kokoscka and another man are with her."

Weber flexed his arms, yawning. He was sleepy but not tired. "Was there any trouble?"

Moreno brushed the crumbs from his jacket. "Not as far as I can understand, sir. The woman was at the lawyer's house. It seems that he insisted on coming here with her."

Weber leaned against the wall. This was definitely not what he wanted.

"Don't tell me he's here!"

Moreno grinned slyly. "Kokoscka made him see reason. The general's return was announced on the ten o'clock news. Paláu says he's going to see him tomorrow."

Weber came upright. "I'll be meeting the general myself. Do you know whether Señora Macneil has gone to bed or not?"

"Her light's still on." Moreno looked back from the window. "She asked when she'd be seeing you, sir."

Weber checked his watch. It was well past midnight. "You'd better go home. Call in at the communications room. I want a call put through to the embassy in Puerto Vedra. Captain Guzman. Get him out of bed if you have to. I'll take the call here in half an hour's time. And no monitoring. The conversation is Top Secret."

He walked through the cloisters to the neighboring

building. What had been a refectory was converted into a small-arms range. The lofty timbered hall stank of burned cordite. Life-size dummies at the end were pitted with bullet holes. The door behind them opened onto a corridor that ran the length of the wing. He came on the first man silently, a youngster with stolid Indian features, sitting on the bottom of the staircase. Weber stepped over his legs, whipping the comic book from the man's lap. Kokoscka heard the noise and came from the shadows at the top of the stairs. Weber threw the comic book at him.

"Pick your men more carefully, Sergeant. I'm making the prisoner your responsibility. Is that understood?"

The look on Kokoscka's face boded no good to his partner. "Yes, sir."

"I want an eight-hour shift," said Weber. "Two men around the clock. Meals will be sent in from the canteen. There's to be no conversation with her and you'll report to me personally."

The chalk-ringed pupils gave Kokoscka's eyes an impression of unwinking perception.

"I'll take a sixteen-hour watch myself, with the colonel's permission. I need very little sleep."

Weber nodded absently. Women prisoners had been held in the new prison at Covaleda for the last five years. The matron's quarters had been unused since then. The ceilings were flaking and the place smelled of mice. He knocked on the bedroom door and turned the key.

An iron cot and bedding had been brought from the guardroom. There was a blue-painted commode and Moreno had found a mirror somewhere. She was standing facing him, her back to the barred window. A green shantung dress camouflaged her swollen stomach. Twin peaks of hair framed slightly prominent cheekbones. The eyes between them were steady. He clicked his heels together, ducking his head.

"My apologies, señora. It was the best we could do at such short notice."

Her voice was calmer than he had expected, more relaxed. "There is something I should make clear, Colonel Weber. The birth of my child is scheduled to be in four weeks' time. Remember that when you are preparing your final excuses."

"We're all very well aware of it, señora. If you feel that you need a doctor at any time, don't hesitate to let us know. Everything will be done for you. Will you please sit down?"

He placed the one chair by the bed, away from the glare of the naked bulb. She moved to it, her face disdainful. She had brought a bag with her. Her sleeping things lay on the pillow. There was a crucifix over the headboard. He could see a toothbrush and sponge in the bathroom. He took her place at the window.

"You look at me with hatred," he said mildly. "Why?"

She covered her throat with her hand, her eyes wide. "You didn't expect approval, surely!"

He shook his head. "I only wanted to point out that I am by no means your enemy. We might as well get the picture clear, señora. I know that your family is well respected. I know that Señor Paláu has influential friends. I am neither an idiot nor a tyrant — just a policeman. But like anyone else, there are times when I find my job distasteful. This is one of them."

"Olé, olé!" Her look was sarcastic. She crossed her ankles. Gold-strapped sandals added to the elegance of her small feet. "It's as well that you mentioned Señor Paláu. I'll tell you something else about him — he happens to be my godfather. You've had me brought here — *bueno!* My place is with my husband anyway. But I hope you understand that it's not just us that you're dealing with. *Do* you understand — or do you actually think that you're above having to justify yourself to anyone?"

A metallic pinging punctuated the silence. It was the faucet dripping into the bathtub. He pushed off the wall, towering to his full height. He made his voice deliberately brutal.

"Your husband's not here, señora. He broke out of the cells with a confederate earlier tonight. They injured one man badly. The other is on the danger list!"

Her fingers flew to her mouth. "I don't believe you," she said, but her eyes were fearful.

He lifted his arms wearily. "What do you want to see — the blood on the floor? You're going to have a baby, Señora Macneil. Take my word for it, everything I've told you is true."

The skin over her cheekbones was stretched and shining. The color had faded beneath her tan. She shook her head slowly.

"I don't believe you. It's a trick. My husband's done nothing. Why should he want to escape?"

He sat down on the bed beside her. "You've just answered your own question. He *had* to escape. The man who went with him is dead. Shot dead a couple of hours ago."

She bent her head quickly so that he could not see her face. Tears trickled through her fingers. He sat quite still, waiting till the fit had passed. She sat up suddenly, pushing the hair from wet distraught eyes.

"What has happened to my husband?"

He spread his hands. "He's known to have crossed the frontier into Puerto Vedra. We know that he's been used in this affair, right from the beginning. He might have been blackmailed for all we know. This much is certain — the dead man was a Castro agent."

"Blackmailed!" she repeated incredulously. She searched his face for an answer. "How *could* he be?"

"A woman, maybe." He said it very casually.

The knuckles of her clenched fists were white. "That's impossible."

"*Is* it?" he asked with meaning. He eased himself up from the bed and stood looking down at her. "I'm not saying that it is a woman. I'm saying that it could have been. We've found out a lot about your husband, señora. He's lied to you about his association with these people. He lied to us about the films he took this morning."

Her eyes never left his for a second. "And what happens now?"

"That's up to him," he said heavily. "His only chance is to cooperate with us. It might even be too late for that. The people he's mixed up with are dangerous. That's why you're here, for protection."

"There's something else," she insisted. "What is it?"

"If we find him, you'd do well to encourage him to return." His eyes were quite steady.

She smiled as if she had just grasped something. "You've overplayed your hand, Colonel. I don't believe in your Castro agents. In fact, I don't believe a single word you've told me, not even about the escape. I *know* my husband. So does Señor Paláu."

Weber's features were rigid. "Then I'll say good night. I'll send some writing material over. If you feel that you need anything, give a note to the guard. Don't waste your time talking to him. You'll find he won't answer."

He turned the key on her. Kokoscka was waiting outside. Weber glanced along the empty corridor. A patch of moonlight spread over the head of the stairs.

"She's all yours," he repeated. "If you want more men, take them."

Kokoscka's smile was perfunctory. "I've got enough, sir. And I'll be here myself. She's hardly likely to be sawing through bars or dropping from windows."

Weber came a couple of steps nearer. He fired the words like bullets. "You take *nothing* for granted. And don't only think of people getting out — think of someone getting *in*."

GENERAL ILIDIO ZUI-MÁRRAGA MINISTER FOR INTERNAL AFFAIRS

HE STOOD at the top of the steps, a fat man with thinning black hair, dressed in a striped Palm Beach suit. His mournful look and hanging wattles gave the impression of a hound dog perturbed by an unfamiliar scent. The heat that came off the cement runway was breathtaking after the cool comfort of the pressurized plane.

He looked down at the ring of waiting officials, shading his eyes. The glare was dazzling in spite of the outsize dark glasses he was wearing. The wind sack over the control tower hung limply. The distant city shimmered like a mirage.

"If the general is ready . . ." the stewardess was smiling at him. Just looking at her gave him a sense of excitement. The smooth coils of hair, plaited like Milanese gold, honeyed skin and a wide mouth that promised sensuality. Her breasts were high and probably firm. Her bottom certainly was. He'd managed to pinch it twice on the jouney from Puerto Vedra. Her telephone number was in his pocket. He tapped her cheek with the tips of his fingers. The fatherly touch was for the benefit of the newsreel cameraman waiting at the bottom of the steps. He winked at the girl on the blind side.

"Adiós, señorita!"

She smiled again, lowering her eyes demurely. Thought of his wife interrupted his pleasure. It was impossible to see the girl in Montoro — would have to be somewhere else — as soon as he could find an excuse. Instinct told him she'd be worth it. He pulled his shoulders back and walked down the steps. The faces around him came into focus. His secretary was there, carrying a bouquet of orchids, no less. As if she was meeting a film star. Idiot. He lifted his arm like a Roman senator, saluting the camera. He reminded himself to have a word with someone at the Ministry of Tourism and Information. They'd been getting far too many shots of his stomach lately.

He made his way through the crowd, distributing nods and handshakes. His secretary was wearing a black dress and shoes. A large cameo brooch hid the cleavage of her breasts decently. He gave her his dispatch case.

"Take good care of that, Señorita Mola!"

There was nothing in it but a copy of *Playboy* and some candy for the children. His papers were with an aide. But it gave her a sense of importance. She smiled nervously.

"Welcome back, General." She had dark hairs on her legs, festooned in nylon sheaths. Like a beetle, he thought with distaste. Thirty-six years and she'd given up. In all probability she'd never started. She was the kind who'd make love with as many clothes on as possible. He smiled at her encouragingly.

"The stomach condition, señorita?" Dyspepsia was an ailment they had in common.

Her sallow skin flushed. "Gracias, Señor General!

Donna Carmen telephoned to say that she will keep the children at home this afternoon. She expects you for lunch."

He heard her with half an ear. He was staring over her shoulder at a black Mercedes drawn up on the tarmac. An enormously tall man was standing in front of it, talking to a group of motorcycle police.

His secretary's voice was hesitant. "Colonel Weber presents his respects. He would like to drive you into the city himself."

Zuimárraga grunted. "I said an escort, not a welcoming committee. What on earth does he want! All right, Señorita Mola — you'd better go on with the others."

He walked across to the waiting German, shielding his head with a newspaper. The uniformed men wheeled away their machines and took up outriders' positions. Two in front, two behind. The stuttering roar of their motorcycles combined with the scream of the jet. The general took Weber's hand, carefully letting his own fingers lie limp. The colonel always insisted on a bone-crushing grip and a penetrating stare. As if one's head literally crawled with guilty secrets. Zuimárraga retrieved his fingers.

"Well now, Weber," he said pacifically. He was fifty pounds overweight and he needed a bath. The thought depressed him. There was something inhuman about the way in which the colonel defied time. The years seemed to leave no mark on him. He climbed into the P.I.D.E. car and fastened the seat belt. He had to move the buckle several inches. Weber was sitting behind the wheel, next to him. The German's scalp glistened healthily through the bristle of iron-gray hair. He smelled of some light, fresh lotion.

Weber's flat-planed face was serious. "I expect you're wondering why I've come myself, sir?"

"Not particularly," Zuimárraga answered. "You've always got a reason even for the most unlikely eventualities." The belt was still cutting into his stomach. He eased it another notch.

"You're going straight home, I take it?"

"I am *not* going straight home," the general said firmly. "Why do you always make these assumptions? I've just returned from an important conference. I have work to do at the ministry. My wife doesn't like this sort of thing anyway. It disturbs the neighbors." He pointed at the outriders.

Weber poked his head through the open window. One of the men in front acknowledged the change in destination. The colonel eased the powerful car forward. The guard at the control-barrier lifted the gate. The cortege rolled out.

"I heard your speech on television, sir," Weber said casually. "It was very convincing."

"Thank you," said the general. The outriders were clearing a way on the fast lane. "That's why we broke up early. There was nothing more to be said." There was an impression of space after Panama. Snow tipped the distant peaks of the Sierra Araña. He put an indigestion tablet on his tongue, suddenly satisfied to be home.

Weber glanced sideways. "I'm sorry to welcome you

with this sort of news, sir. The fact is, we've discovered a Castro ring operating in the city. I think you'll understand why I didn't call you in Panama."

The General's molars crunched hard on the peppermint. He saw himself rising at the conference table, Balboa Park and the bay beyond the enormous windows. The rows of attentive faces as his resonant phrases rolled off, one after another.

I have listened with interest to the reports of the distinguished delegates. My own case is embarrasingly simple. In Montoro we have no Cuban problem. What has been our safeguard is a wedding of enlightened thought and our Catholic heritage.

"A *ring?*" he repeated incredulously. His voice cracked. He lowered it, irritated. The word bothered him as much as the context. "How many, for God's sake — ten, fifty, a thousand?"

Weber took his eyes off the road for a second. "The nucleus of a ring, anyway, sir. Two men."

The general cleared the last shreds of peppermint from his gums. "Why do you always have to dramatize things, Weber?" The question sounded petulant and he knew it.

"I'm not aware that I do," the colonel replied. "I had news last week that a man would be arriving, a Castro agent. He's not even a Cuban but a Jew. The name on his passport was Asher. Not that this meant anything. The passport was American and false. We know that he spent two years in Havana and was trained in East Germany. There's no doubt that he was here to organize cells. His contact was a Canadian who's a resident in the city. We arrested them both yesterday."

"Well thank God for that," Zuimárraga felt as if he'd been sandbagged. His brain was dull and unreceptive. He was only too conscious of the other man's contempt. Much of it was based on jealousy. As a foreigner, the German could never go any higher than he already had. And as a policeman he was in a class of his own.

Weber overtook a bus top-heavy with chicken crates. "They both escaped from headquarters last night. The Canadian managed to cross the border into Puerto Vedra. The Jew was shot dead, near Frente Rio."

Zuimárraga allowed his sarcasm to be obvious. "Well at least you keep to the formula, Weber."

The German's voice was stiffly correct. "I'm not too sure that I understand, sir."

Zuimárraga crossed his short arms on his chest. "If my memory is correct, you have lost five arrests in the past two years. All of them were shot dead while trying to escape."

Weber was poker-faced at the wheel. "One of them committed suicide," he corrected.

Zuimárraga made a sound of disgust. "Is that meant to be humorous? Let me remind you of a statement you made at a presidential commission no longer ago than four months. 'The Police in the Defense of the State has outgrown its image of terror.' "

Weber swerved to pass a truck. "I'll admit that your own caption was better, sir. 'A finger on the pulse of the nation.' I lack that sort of imagination."

Zuimárraga shifted uneasily. "All right, I might as well hear the rest of it."

Weber's eyes were on the road ahead. They were rapidly nearing the outskirts of the city.

"You were in Panama. I hardly wanted to bring it up on the phone. I knew this Jew was supposed to be meeting his contact on the hippodrome. I had the whole area sealed off. Then at the last minute I decided to arrest them separately. It was a mistake and I admit it. The Canadian had time to see his wife. You'll be getting a visit from a lawyer called Paláu."

"*Gregorio* Paláu!" The general groaned. "Couldn't you have picked on someone else? The man's dynamite."

The motorcycles in front wheeled in unison, cutting off the traffic from the coming intersection. The cortege sliced through.

"I had no choice," Weber said dryly. He drove like a European, defensively. "I only found out who he was an hour ago. The trouble is that he thinks his client is innocent. The Canadian's no fool. He'd managed to hoodwink everyone, including his wife. She's at San Vincente, incidentally. I arrested her, too."

Wind rumbled in the general's gut. "What do you mean 'incidentally,' man? If she believes her husband to be innocent, what's the charge?"

"There isn't one, sir." Weber's tone was matter-of-fact. "She's being held in safe custody."

"Mother of God," Zuimárraga wheezed. His mind was on a cocoloco. Several of them in fact, drunk one after the other. Tall glasses of chilled coconut-milk laced with rum.

95

Weber threw the next lines away almost indifferently. "She's a Montoresa and heavily pregnant. Her husband's only a hundred-and-sixty kilometers away."

The general's jowls quivered. He steadied himself against the lurch of the car.

"Don't you have any scruples at all, Colonel?"

"Not in this sort of thing," Weber said shortly.

It was some time before Zuimárraga could bring himself to speak again.

"This is all very interesting but what am I supposed to do? I can't very well ignore someone of Paláu's caliber. I'll have to see him, you realize that?"

"Naturally, sir. But only see him once. Cast me as the villain if you like. You're deeply sympathetic but the matter's out of your hands."

"I'm beginning to think it is," Zuimárraga offered grimly.

Weber shrugged. "It's probable that Paláu will mention a camera. The Canadian took one up to the racetrack. We made a fuss about it purposely but it has no real bearing."

They were into the city now, weaving through the narrow streets of the Old City. The smell of rotting fruit and fish was familiar. The general spoke from a strong feeling of indignation.

"You say this man's known to be in Puerto Vedra. Isn't there something that can be done at that end?"

"We're doing something, sir." Weber turned his head slightly. "I'd sooner you don't ask any more questions for obvious reasons. The less you know, the less you feel obliged to disclose."

The general muttered under his breath. It was an interesting suggestion. He knew exactly what Weber meant. The report to the president was scheduled for Monday. The phrases delivered in Panama rolled again.

"I don't think I know anything," he said carefully. "Not at this stage, anyway."

"There's no need, sir." Weber's assurance was comforting. "There never was any need. But I had to put you in the picture."

The general grunted again. That much at least was true. There was no mention of the way Weber intended dealing with the Canadian. Nothing specific. It was better to leave the German with a completely free hand. The ploy had paid off in the past. The avenue was shaded by venerable plane trees. The ministry was an untidy building with a pink plaster front. It covered the entire block. A line of official cars was parked in front of it.

Zuimárraga unfastened his seat belt. "Let me out here. I'll go in through the side entrance."

Weber braked to the curb. "You might let me know what happens with Paláu, sir. It just might be useful."

The general lumbered out. Sudden movements of any kind left him increasingly breathless. Weight, again. He'd really have to do something about dieting. He leaned back through the window on Weber's side, struck by an afterthought.

"Peculiar. I've never known you concerned about a lawyer before."

The German's expression was impassive. "We haven't had a Communist cell before."

Zuimárraga withdrew his head sharply. "You're not suggesting Paláu is part of it."

"I'm suggesting he doesn't believe in it," Weber said steadily. "Whose side does that put him on?"

The general nodded good-bye. "I'll keep you informed," he promised. He went through a small iron gate, cut across the grass to an obscure door at the end of the building. A double twist of his key neutralized the electronic warning system. His heavy tread made no sound on the thickly carpeted corridor. Two more doors let him into the main part of the ministry. The passages and elevators linking the seventy-four rooms were patroled by a closed TV circuit. Control posts were placed at each of the four main entrances. Weber had designed the system. Zuimárraga despised it. The German's insistence on gadgets was almost American. The real key to security lay in the understanding of human motives, not in a panel of lighted buttons. He opened another door, pleased with the thought.

The great hall was open to its painted ceiling. He climbed a staircase to a room framed in damask wallpaper. The furniture and beams were somber. Red velvet curtains cascaded over deeply recessed windows. An oil painting of a thickset man in admiral's uniform hung above the mantel. Zuimárraga eased himself behind his desk. The silver frame in front of him showed a snapshot of a woman and two children. Her face was almost Madonna-like. The girls were seated in her voluminous lap. He put the air hostess's telephone number away in a drawer. An aide answered his summons.

The young man was smart in sand-colored breeches and riding boots. Captain's tabs gleamed in his freshly ironed shirt. Zuimárraga waved his hand at the empty desk.

"*Muy buenas,* Carlos! Does this mean there's no work for me — too good to be true!"

The young man's pleasure was obvious. "There was nothing that Señorita Mola and I couldn't handle between us, General. But I'm afraid you do have a visitor. He's been waiting here for over an hour — a Supreme Court lawyer called Paláu."

"Show him in," said Zuimárraga. He molded his fat cheeks into a welcoming smile as the door opened.

Paláu entered like a cat reconnoitering an unfamiliar alley. He was elegant in snakeskin shoes and a silk suit. His thin brown face was intelligent under prematurely white hair. He wasted no time.

"It's good of you to see me, Excellency. I apologize for not asking for an appointment. The matter is extremely urgent."

Zuimárraga waved him into a chair. "I knew your father. It would be difficult for me to refuse to see a Paláu."

The lawyer's acknowledgment was perfunctory. "I'd better warn you, General — you won't like what I have to say. I can only ask you to hear me out."

The general pushed his wife's picture out of the way. It was blocking his view of the lawyer's face.

"I'll tell you something in confidence, Counselor. Not much that I hear in this room does give me pleasure. The next half-hour is at your disposal."

Paláu's hand moved from side to side. "Five minutes

99

should be enough. A Canadian citizen called Dougal Macneil was arrested by P.I.D.E. yesterday. The pretense is that he was in a prohibited area with a camera. His wife was arrested eight hours later — at gunpoint in the house of my mother. Both these people are my clients. Colonel Weber refuses to let me see them. Point number one."

Zuimárraga's jowls quivered. "Am I to take it there are more?"

"Point number two," Paláu continued calmly. "Señora Macneil is a Montoresan citizen. She's married to a Canadian but she's still a citizen as far as we're concerned. Her maiden name was Najaras y Ortega. Point number three — she is pregnant. I can vouch for this couple personally, General. I know them both intimately. Señora Macneil is my goddaughter."

"I don't know if you're aware of it," protested the general. "But I've been out of the country for almost two weeks. In fact, I only arrived back from Panama three quarters of an hour ago. I've had no time to see any reports. Where exactly are your clients now?"

Paláu released a thin stream of smoke at the ceiling. "Where P.I.D.E. usually holds its prisoners — in San Vincente."

Zuimárraga brooded behind clasped hands. "Let's get our facts right, Counselor. Your clients have been taken into custody and you don't know why — is that it?"

Paláu's quick look was sardonic. "We both know that the director of P.I.D.E. is not obliged to give reasons. Colonel Weber is too much the policeman to volunteer information. But the suggestion is that in some mysterious way, Macneil has been conspiring against the State. If this is true, Weber needs his head examined."

Zuimárraga wheezed out of his chair reluctantly. "I think your zeal is running away with you, Señor Paláu. Let me be the judge of the colonel's sanity. I appreciate your concern for your clients and I'm glad that you came to see me. Rest assured that I shall ask for a full report."

Paláu spoke deliberately. "There's one thing I haven't mentioned. Señora Macneil is eight months pregnant. Do you realize what it could mean, confining a woman in her condition?"

The thought did nothing for Zuimárraga's peace of mind. He tried to convince himself.

"Everything will be done for her comfort. You have my word for it."

The lawyer rose. He paused at the door. "You won't give me an order to see them at least once. Señora Macneil, *surely?*"

"I'm sorry, Counselor." The general's manner was regretful. "But I cannot interfere with Colonel Weber's decisions. Adiós."

As soon as the door shut he touched a bell. His aide answered it. "I don't want to see that man again, Carlos. Not for any reason. If he comes back or telephones for an appointment, I'm not available. Now get me a car. I'm going home."

It was ten hours later when he opened a cautious eye, coming out of his doze. The awning was swinging in the slight breeze. A faint smell of carameled lemon peel drifted into the patio. Behind the kitchen door, the maid was clattering crockery. His wife's chair was close to the children's window. Her voice trailed on through his drowsiness, fond and indulgent.

"That's enough, children. Papa's resting. Go to sleep."

He opened the other eye resignedly. Carmen's face made an ivory oval in the twilight. The smooth cap of hair was as black as the dress she was wearing. It was always black somehow. Married women over thirty-five seemed to wear it as if wedlock were a form of suicide. Fourteen years had changed the once willowy body into a mound of flesh as ponderous as his own. Nothing remained of the sparkling bride but the delicate ankles and an occasional flash of spirit. Even that was rare, he thought morosely. They both ate far too much. He remembered the girl on the plane and the fantasy saddened him with its implications. He was fifty-seven years of age, balding and dyspeptic. He'd never see her again, of course. The whole thing had been no more than an academic exercise in virility.

His wife's voice restored reality. The flower in her hair pinpointed her face in the dark.

"Father Loyola telephoned."

He stretched his arms, yawning. The palace chaplain was quick off the mark as always. Convention required attendance at Easter Sunday Mass. The presidential staff appeared in full-dress uniform. Ministers wore tail suits. Confessions were heard on the Saturday. Father Loyola's penances seemed to grow longer with the years.

He lit a cigarette. "I was thinking of asking God to excuse me this time."

His wife made a sound of disapproval. "Don't be irreligious."

He pitched the spent match at the base of the hibiscus tree. "I'm not."

His wife reached up and rapped on the window sharply. The giggling inside the room stopped.

"Does that mean you're not going to confession?" she demanded.

He looked up at the sky, a glitter of tiny points of light. "It means that after forty-seven years of it God might be getting tired of Ilidio Zuimárraga's confidences."

She was quiet for a moment before making her next assault. "There's something troubling you, Ilidio. What is it?"

The suggestion irritated him as always. The wish to invade the privacy of his mind. Carmen never accepted that only part of his life was hers — as only part of it belonged to his daughters. What she required was totality. He changed the subject.

"Were you afraid when you were pregnant, Carmen? I mean with Maribel?"

She smoothed her skirt placidly. "Aiee, afraid! No, I wasn't. None of us knew that I was going to have a caesarean, remember — not even Doctor Galvez. It was too late to be afraid by then. I didn't feel a thing, anyway. What makes you ask such a strange question?"

Zuimárraga's head drooped. He was thinking of the wound that scarred her belly — rubber-gloved hands reaching into her womb to give life to their firstborn.

"I have to go out," he said suddenly. "You go to bed."

She rose, her face and voice tranquil. "Where else would I go?" she asked quietly.

The remark revived his irritation. He opened the door for her. The big living room was pleasantly furnished. Carmen's silver reflected the soft candlelight. Toys littered the floor. Rugs had been draped across chairs to form a tent. He straightened them mechanically.

"What happens when I'm away?" he asked sourly. "You don't sit alone. Why don't you call one of your friends — there's a telephone."

She smiled patiently. "It's your first night at home. I wouldn't want people to know that you're not spending it with your family."

The riposte found him vulnerable. "I won't be more than an hour. There's something I have to do."

Her eyes were understanding. "Then do it, *querido*. Wake me if I'm asleep."

He left the house through the front door. A dense hedge lined with flowerbeds protected the lawn from the road. A man moved from the veranda. Zuimárraga motioned him into the garage.

"We're going to P.I.D.E. headquarters, Gonzalez."

A string of colored lanterns hung in the garden opposite. He heard a girl's laughter, the sound of a guitar. He released the hand brake, letting the car roll out onto the road. There were matrons on the porch, their fans fluttering like moths' wings. Carmen could easily have joined them. But no, a man had to be made to feel guilty.

He parked on the square on top of the hill. The courtyard was illuminated like a film set. The trees, fountain and guardroom were stark under the harshness of arc lamps. They seemed to be expecting visitors. Zuimárraga rang the bell. A man peered through the gate, he unfastened it hurriedly, recognizing his caller. The general strolled across to the guardhouse. The room was still ringing with laughter. The duty officer detached himself from a group of men, snapping a hasty salute.

There was something about San Vincente that had always bothered the general. Even in broad daylight he found himself thinking about the dungeons under the drowsy gardens. Relics of the Inquisition. The uneasiness was based on a childhood memory. He still dreamed of being trapped in a cellar, forgotten for hours, small fists beating on the door in a frenzy of fear.

"Is Colonel Weber in the building?" he asked.

The duty officer's face was regretful. "The colonel left an hour ago, Excellency. Captain Moreno is still in his office. Shall I tell him you're here?"

Zuimárraga shook his head. That was something else about San Vincente — the reminder that it was Weber who commanded.

"I understand you have a female prisoner," he said smoothly. "I'd like to see her."

The duty officer stiffened. The men behind him were suddenly conspicuously busy.

"Colonel Weber left orders that the woman is to receive no visitors, Excellency. *Perdón.*"

"Pardon is for Christ on the Cross." The general inspected the man from head to foot. "Where is this prisoner, Lieutenant?"

Caution invaded the man's answer. "In the old matron's quarters, Excellency. Behind the practice range. Shall I send someone with you?"

"You've done your duty," Zuimárraga answered. "Go back to your work."

The cloisters were dark and silent. Moonlight silvered the grass between them. He walked the length of the armory wing. A patch of yellow showed behind the barred windows overhead. The door in front of him was unlocked. He was almost at the top of the stairs when a bare bulb came on in the ceiling. A man stepped into the light, barring the general's way to the landing.

Zuimárraga leaned against the banister, catching his breath. "Do you know who I am?" he gasped.

The guard was in his forties, a foreigner from his accent. His eyes bore the glare without blinking.

"I know, Excellency," he said with respect. He still barred the way to the rooms behind him.

The general climbed the last two steps. "Your name?" he wheezed.

The man's manner was deferential but determined. "Sergeant Kokoscka, Excellency. The Señor General will excuse me but I cannot let anyone pass. I am responsible to Colonel Weber in person."

"Kokoscka," the general repeated thoughtfully. The sergeant was obviously one of Weber's Praetorian Guard. He covered his discomfiture with a show of good humor. "You're quite right, Sergeant. I'll see the Colonel myself. Good night."

The man transferred his gun to his left hand and saluted. He kept the light on till the general reached the bottom of the stairs. Then he snapped it off, leaving the landing in darkness. Zuimárraga looked back as he walked across the grass. A woman's face showed briefly at the upstairs window, then the curtains were drawn. Weber's office was empty. The door to the adjoining room was open. He peered in.

"Ah, Moreno! Tell me, Captain, do you happen to know where Colonel Weber is?"

He read the truth on Moreno's foxy face. No one here was likely to give him a straight answer. The realization made him uncomfortable. He should never have come here in the first place. It was Weber's affair. Interference could only be dangerous.

"Never mind," he put in quickly. "Just ask him to phone me first thing in the morning."

DOUGAL MACNEIL

Tʜᴇ ʙᴜs from Chiclana limped the last few kilometers, coming in on the new Centenary Bridge. There was a clear view of the city over the oil tankers and banana boats. It was barely nine o'clock. Downtown Puerto Vedra had all the extravagance of Southern California. Tall skyscrapers clustered in the early-morning sunshine. Waving coconut palms fringed the waterfront. The white towers and pipelines of the oil-cracking plant looked like parts of some giant chemistry set. A streak of vapor trailed behind a jet planing in overhead. The twenty-million-dollar air terminal and the status of a free port had sucked new wealth into the tiny republic. Bank charters went for a thousand dollars. International corporations flocked in to benefit from tax concessions.

A backwash of the dispossessed followed as doors slammed on them all over the world. Five percent of the population was stateless. Deserters from a dozen lost causes lived there precariously, bringing old skills to new occupations. Catalonian Anarchists mixed with refugee Nazis, an improbable colony of Hungarians was still loyal to Admiral Horthy. The more prosperous were those who had become shallow-water smugglers. Fast boats ran duty-free goods the length of the Caribbean. The more troubled in spirit drifted from bar to bar, peddling peach-stone carvings and pot. For these, hope was a word that meant that tomorrow you ate.

Macneil dropped off near the Stock Exchange Building. The sun struck relentlessly, reflecting from the banked windows on the eastern side of the edifice. He ducked into the narrow street behind. Every other doorway bore a money changer's shingle. He surrendered Asher's pesos for Puerto Vedran currency. He put the bills in his pocket. The gun made a conspicuous bulge beneath his belt. Three hundred and sixty-four dollars seemed little enough to bankroll a caper like Asher's, whatever it had been.

He walked a couple of blocks north into an area of wide streets, and plate-glass towers. Water spouted in fountains, spilled into terraced pools. It was Good Friday but elegant-fronted stores still offered Italian leather, French scents, cashmere sweaters from the Burlington Arcade. The jewelers' boutiques were small but their windows blazed with diamonds. Beside this Montoro was no more than a provincial capital. Tiles set in the sidewalk advertised the corner building.

ALMACENES DE REFORMA   CENTRAL AMERICA'S LARGEST
DEPARTMENT STORE

It was cool inside. The salesclerks behind the counters were still half-asleep, moving languorously to the sound of piped music. He bought himself a wash-and-wear suit in light gray material, putting it on in the change room. The

109

gun was well hidden now beneath his jacket. He left his dirty jeans behind, adding shirts, a razor and toothbrush to his purchases. He left the store carrying a small canvas bag. He took it into a neighboring barbershop and dropped into a vacant chair. Steamed towels eased the fatigue from his eyes. He'd spent the night in a dogwood patch, emerging to catch the first bus out of the border village. The shoeshine boy's rag slapped the new loafers to a dazzling polish.

Macneil wiped his face, looking at himself in the mirror. The lines from his nose to mouth might have been scored by the barber's razor. He knotted the string tie and gave the man a bill. A cab was cruising by. He flagged it down and leaned back against the hot vinyl.

"Hotel Toledo, Plaza de Insurgentes."

The hack drove in Puerto Vedran fashion, one hand permanently depressing the horn ring. He passed on the right or left, wherever a gap presented itself in the traffic. The narrow street ahead slowed him to a crawl that he suffered impatiently. Store windows were filled with the junk of four continents. Music blared from bar doorways. The faded awnings above them were descriptive.

BRÜDERSCHAFT BIERKELLER   HANK'S LAST HOPE
BAR DE LA RÉVOLUTION BASQUE

A dingy four-storied building dominated the square at the heart of things. Horse-drawn carriages stood in the shadow of the palms. The ears of the animals poked through straw hats. The driver braked flamboyantly. He looked back, showing a mouthful of tobacco-stained teeth.

110

"Hotel Toledo, señor!"

Macneil ran up the steps. He and Pilar had stayed there a dozen times over the years. The rooms were clean and cheap. No food was served but the square had half a dozen restaurants. The desk clerk was familiar, a sullen-faced refugee from the Budapest uprising. He greeted Macneil in English.

"Good morning, sir. The señora is not with you this time?"

Macneil shook his head. "Not for the moment. She'll be joining me later." If ever there was wishful thinking that was it. Nothing seemed to have changed, from the ancient bullfight posters to the out-of-order sign on the elevator cage.

The clerk slid a form in the Canadian's direction. His eyebrows made a solid bar of coarse black hair that was reproduced on his upper lip.

"If you'll just fill this in, sir, and let me have your passport."

The form was standard. Name, age, number of passport, nationality. "I'll do that later," Macneil said easily. "I'd like a room on the top floor, at the front."

There was a subtle change in the clerk's manner. "I'm afraid I'll have to ask you to do it now, sir. We're not allowed to register guests without first seeing the identification papers."

Macneil completed the form and glanced up. "I can't remember the number of my passport. I left it at the consulate on my way up here. I'll collect it later. What is this, anyway — we're in Puerto Vedra."

The desk clerk spread his hands. "It's a new regulation, sir. It started a couple of months ago. The International Police collect these forms every evening and they check the passports. I can't give you a key. I'm sorry. But I have my job to think about."

Macneil ripped the form into small pieces. He leaned over the counter and dropped them into the trashbasket. The clerk said he worried. Maybe he did but the chances were that he'd left a wife and family behind in Budapest. Did he worry about *them?* The first people to run were always those that a country could do without anyway. Giving the guy money was useless. He was the kind of creep who'd take a bribe and then holler for the law.

"Listen to me," he said deliberately. "I told you — you'll get the passport later. I'll fill in another form then. In the meantime there's no law against my leaving my bag upstairs." He held his hand out.

The clerk surrendered a room key reluctantly. "It's not me, you'll understand, sir. It's the police. You have to see my position."

Macneil picked up his bag. "There's no problem. I'll probably be staying for a week. I'll know just as soon as my wife joins me. Find out what the delay is on a call to Ciudad de Montoro."

The fifth-floor room had an iron bed with legs set in ant-proof water containers. It was draped in mosquito netting. There was a telephone and a Gideon Bible in Spanish on the table. A smell of stale scent hung in the clothes closet. He threw the windows wide. Tourists were drinking beer on the sidewalk across the square. Dogs lay inert in the gathering heat. Flat roofs stepped the rising ground to the north. Bougainvillea splashed the tops of the houses purple and mauve. The dome of the ayuntamiento bulged on the skyline like an inflamed bunion. The address that was etched on his memory lay somewhere beneath it. Asher's last thought had been for that scrap of paper. Macneil's hunch told him that the address was in some way connected with his own arrest. Whoever he found there was going to have some explaining to do.

This business with the desk clerk meant an alteration in his schedule however. It had to be the consul first, now. Then the photographs. Shashoua came last of all. He locked the gun with his bag in the clothes closet and pocketed the key. The corridors were strangely quiet. The lobby was still empty except for the clerk. Macneil's inquiry was casual.

"Am I alone in the place?"

The Hungarian hung the key on the board. His manner was ungracious. "They come and they go. About your call to Ciudad de Montoro. They say there's a three-hour delay. Do you still want me to book the call or not?"

There was something resentful in the clerk's face. As if Macneil had fallen short in some way or other. The Canadian scribbled Paláu's home and office numbers on a pad.

"Book them both — make the call person-to-person. I might try myself from downtown. If I manage to get through I'll phone you."

Fate had pitched him into a strange new world of subtle fears and values. Even the commonplace had to be seen in new perspective. A sudden knock on the door — the way he spoke on the phone — a stranger's request for a light. And for the moment, it was Weber who had all the marbles.

The consulate was downtown in a building only three blocks from the photography store. Fountains ringed the concourse in front of it. The lavish use of water cooled the surrounding air. He rode the express elevator to the top floor. The big bright reception room overlooked the busy avenue. None of its noise disturbed the ordered calm. A girl with a boyish crop and an openwork blouse looked up from her magazine.

He nodded greeting. "I'm Dougal Macneil. I'd like to see the consul."

Her manner was a tribute to some prairie-province school of business. A diversionary feint followed the quick keen assessment.

"I'm afraid the consul's busy at the moment, Mr. Macneil. Would you like to see his assistant?"

He took the chair beside her. "Let's get this much straight, it's the consul himself I want."

She crossed tanned legs and decided to smile. "That's just not possible, Mr. Macneil. It's Good Friday. We're only open till noon. He's got a whole book full of appointments today. Mr. Poirier's taking all the unscheduled business."

He leaned sideways behind a pointed finger. "Look, young lady, I'm not trying to make things difficult for you but this is something I have to discuss with the consul himself. If he's busy I'll wait. And I *will* wait," he added significantly.

Her cheeks colored. "Just a minute."

He sat there alone, staring at the posters that decorated the walls. An R.C.M.P. sergeant invited the world to see Canada first. The green lakes of the Rockies shone like emeralds. Middle-aged men in waders smiled from the middle of salmon streams. The girl was back in the doorway, beckoning.

"Do you want to come through, Mr. Macneil?"

He followed her into the inner room. The man standing by the window had a corded neck and freckles. His hands were gripping the lapels of his white jacket. The fact that he kept his pipe in his mouth gave his speech a certain severity.

"My name is Lester Pollard. What can I do for you, Mr. Macneil?"

There was a desk with a couple of telephones, a battery of pens and pencils. A small Canadian flag on a base served as paperweight. A picture of the queen hung over a bookcase.

"I don't have my passport," Macneil said bluntly. "The police in Montoro confiscated it yesterday."

The consul removed his pipe. His jaw was no less stern without it.

"Sit down, will you." He frowned across the desk, creaking back in his chair. "Montoro, you say. Then how did you get here?"

"I walked over the frontier at Chiclana," Macneil answered steadily. "You'd better hear the rest of it. I was up on the racetrack . . ." Talked out like this, the whole business seemed even more fantastic. He withheld two facts. The truth about the films and the address he had taken from the dead Jew. Instinct told him he was right. What he had said was enough for his purpose.

Pollard sucked away at his pipe, his gray eyes growing more skeptical by the minute.

"All right," he said when Macneil was done. "Let me recap your story. You are an escaped prisoner who has come into Puerto Vedra illegally. And you're expecting me to bail you out, right?"

Macneil looked at him blankly. The guy was even smiling. "I'm expecting you to give me help," he said doggedly. "Some sort of identification at least."

Pollard tapped his pipe out, shaking his head. "Your ideas of consular procedure seem to me to be pretty naive. Let's start at square one. You say you're a Canadian citizen — what proof are you offering?"

"Why don't you call the consulate in Ciudad de Montoro?" Macneil put in quickly. "They know me there."

Pollard pressed a buzzer. A younger man poked his head around the door.

"Get Montoro on the line," the consul said smoothly. "Make it priority." He thought for a moment. "We still won't be sure that *you* are Dougal Macneil."

Macneil struggled to control himself but his voice shook. "You must be putting me on! What do you want, fingerprints? I'm sorry, I never had mine taken."

Pollard held up a warning hand. "Hold it, before you say the wrong thing! What I'm trying to do is get you straightened out. OK. P.I.D.E. picked you up and all the rest of it. You're *still* in this country illegally. If you want anything from me, you'll have to surrender yourself to the police first."

The bookshelves dragged Macneil's attention like a magnet. It was all there, he thought helplessly. Regulations governing treatment of a man in deep trouble. Article one: Make sure you put him in deeper. He jumped as the phone rang.

Pollard answered. "Harry? — Lester. Look I've got someone here who claims you know him. Dougal Macneil — that's right, ten minutes ago. I see."

He cradled the phone between his shoulder and cheek, freeing his hands to relight his pipe. His interruptions were brief and noncommittal. He finally put the phone down.

"Didn't you say that your wife was staying with your lawyer?"

Macneil moved his head. "She was going to his mother — Donna Rafaela Paláu — why?"

A new concern clouded the consul's eyes. "She's been arrested by P.I.D.E. Your lawyer reported it to my colleague late last night."

The news sandbagged its way into Macneil's brain. "But she's eight months pregnant!"

"Yeah, well let's think." Pollard scribbled something on the pad in front of him. "You're right," he said quietly, looking up. "You're in real trouble. You know this P.I.D.E. outfit better than I do. The only information they'll release is that you were arrested and escaped. They say your wife's in protective custody. I've got some advice for you from the consul in Montoro."

"Advice?" Macneil said stupidly.

"It's the same as mine," Pollard told him. "Turn yourself in. There's no extradition treaty between this country and Montoro for nonnationals. You're lucky."

Macneil's face flushed. "Did you say *lucky?*"

Pollard's pipe conducted an unseen orchestra. "I'll have to get in touch with Ottawa first. They'll probably want me to go to the police with you. Where are you staying?"

A metronome ticked warningly in Macneil's mind. "Nowhere. I came straight here. I guess you're right. What else *can* I do — How long have I got?"

"Good man!" Pollard's manner was that of a hockey coach congratulating a successful rookie. He shrugged. "There's no hurry now we've made our minds up. It might even be tomorrow morning before I get a signal back from Ottawa. You'll need a place to sleep."

Macneil nodded. It was half-past ten. Twenty-four hours in which to set up his return to Montoro.

"I'll try the Toledo in the Barrio Viejo. I've stayed there before. They're bound to want some sort of identification."

"Tell 'em to get in touch with us," the consul said easily. He circled the desk and wrapped an arm around Macneil's shoulder. He walked him as far as the door.

"Don't worry about your wife. As soon as P.I.D.E. knows that you're here, they'll let her go. The Puerto Vedran authorities aren't likely to hold you long — a couple of weeks at the most. Give me a ring, first thing in the morning."

Macneil left the building with an odd calm — as if the

moment were some long-awaited anticlimax. Weber *wanted* him back in Montoro. The trap was set and he was supposed to walk right into it. But even a rat grew cunning enough to snatch the bait without springing the lever. He crossed the concourse and headed for the photographer's shop. It was a modern store in the middle of a busy block. A sign over the end counter read DEVELOPING. The salesclerk had on a surgery-type white jacket. He took Macneil's name and riffed through the contents of a drawer. He checked a yellow envelope and smiled.

"Transparencies, right, señor? If you'd like to have a look at them." He indicated an enlarger and snapped the light on for Macneil.

The Canadian fed the slides into the machine. The camera lens had caught what his eye had missed. The front end of a police jeep showed near the pari-mutuels. The two men must have watched him walk across from the finishing post. The fourth, fifth and sixth slides were the important ones. He blew them up to the limit and peered into the viewer. The fast shutter speed had frozen three men in front of the helicopter. The colors were true, the definition excellent. The youngest of the trio stood a few feet away from the others. Khaki drills and a pair of goggles identified him as the pilot. The second man was Weber, tall and unsmiling. He seemed to be pointing at the distant mountains with his right arm. The man he was talking to was in his sixties and wore a stained white suit. The next shot showed him with his hat off. His head was partly bald. A hand shielded his eyes and fleshy nose. He had a hard mouth and fleshy jowls. There was a coarseness about the face, a look of sullen brutality that belonged to a skid-row bartender.

Macneil put the slides and negatives back in the envelope and paid for them. Just *having* them gave him a feeling of confidence. They linked him to Weber and because of Weber to Pilar. Whether the links reached Shashoua remained to be seen. He walked out into the dazzling sunshine. The nearest cab stand was fifty yards north. He kept to the outside edge of the sidewalk, jostling his way through the crowd. One hand held the envelope tight in his pocket. For the moment at least he was safe. His senses seemed to be on stalks, pushing out in every direction. He passed the line of parked cars, still thinking about Shashoua. The name was no more than part of an address but he had to play his hunch. Pilar was in a police cell and time running out on him. He climbed into the first cab and gave the driver the hotel address.

An elderly woman was reading a newspaper in the lobby. Macneil retrieved his key. The desk clerk's eyes were curious but he said nothing. Macneil found a chamber maid on the top floor, working her way down with a mop and pail. He let himself into his room and took the gun from the clothes closet. He waited at the door till he heard the maid going down the stairs. There was a tiny room at the end of the corridor, not much bigger than a cupboard. The shelves inside were piled with sheets and blankets. He hauled himself up on the bottom rack. He could just reach the ledge overhead. He pulled down a shoe box. It was covered in dust and empty. He hid the gun and transparencies in it and climbed down again. The box was out of sight from the floor.

Back in his room, he splashed his face and hands with water. He left the clothes closet unlocked. He surrendered his key to the Hungarian at the reception desk.

"The Canadian consulate will be calling. Tell them I'm registering."

The clerk's eyebrows shifted. "I just this minute did it. They were on the line while you were upstairs."

"Did they mention the passport?" Macneil asked easily.

The clerk nodded. "They mentioned it. How about this call to Montoro. Do you want that canceled or not?"

Macneil eyed him cautiously. The guy's manner was suddenly knowing — as if a nose familiar with the furtive had sniffed out his guest's secret.

"Keep it in the pipe," he said. "I'll be back."

He stood at the top of the hotel steps and called a carriage over. The driver nodded at Macneil's question. The Canadian settled back in leather redolent of the stables. The tourists were on their third or fourth iced beer. Not a head turned as the carriage rounded the square. It was a foolproof way to throw off a tail, he thought confidently. Another carriage or a car slowed to their pace would be conspicuous. The streets narrowed as they climbed into the Barrio Viejo. Finally there were no sidewalks. The gray's hooves struck sparks from the cobblestones. Its nervous ears were grotesque in the straw hat. The driver was having difficulty keeping the animal on its feet. He reined in suddenly.

"It's as far as I go, señor."

Macneil continued on foot. The alleys reeked of ammonia. Predatory cats stalked among the garbage. Sewing machines clattered behind beaded doorways to the tinny accompaniment of transistors. The Chinese sweatshops ran a twelve-hour service in Palm Beach suits for the tourists. He turned a corner. The street came to an abrupt end twenty yards away, blocked by a wall. The bulbous dome of the ayuntamiento poked over the top of it. Kids were playing at the base of the wall. The sun beat down on the tightly shuttered windows of a whorehouse. A drunk lay there where he had fallen, his head on the steps. Flies buzzed over the bloodstains around him. The last house on the left was distinguished by blue-washed walls. Dwarf jacarandas grew outside a door covered with a metal grille. A sign was let into a tile.

BENJAMIN SHASHOUA   EXPORT AND IMPORT

He pushed the door open. It closed behind him, shutting out the shrill shrieks of the children. The thick white-washed walls were decorated with Japanese flower prints. Esparto matting covered the floor. The table and chairs were made of cane. The only apparent concession to business was a collection of samples on a display stand. The big room was cool and empty. He walked to a bead-hung archway. His voice echoed down the passage beyond.

"Olá!"

He whirled as a door opened at the far end of the room. The woman standing there was tall and light-haired. A white sleeveless dress accentuated her thin arms and flat chest. She was about thirty with an earnest scholarly manner.

"*Guten Morgen,*" she said, inspecting Macneil. "*Was soll ich für Sie?*"

He shook his head. "I don't speak German. I'd like to see Mr. Shashoua. My name is Macneil."

Her English accent was labored. "Mr. Shashoua is not here. I am Frau Hoenigsberg. Can I help you?"

"When do you expect Mr. Shashoua?" he demanded.

She pulled a strand of hair into place, avoiding his eyes. "It is difficult to say. He is absent on business. Perhaps if you leave a message . . ."

Her body was inclined toward the open door behind her. He had the impression that someone was behind it. He raised his tone. "You can tell him Philip Asher sent me."

She smiled vaguely but her manner told him that he was right about one thing. Someone *was* listening. She pushed one of the cane chairs toward him.

"Please — I shall make an inquiry."

He could see the street from where he sat. It was oddly still. He realized that the children had gone. The drunk had fallen down a couple of steps and was lying on his back. Macneil swiveled his head slowly. He had a strong feeling that he was being watched. It was some time before the woman reappeared. She fluttered her fingers at him, smiling again.

"Come, please."

Beyond the door was a short staircase. Brass treads glittered in the dragon-patterned carpet. The woman pointed, nodding encouragingly.

"Mr. Shashoua."

He climbed the stairs to a room full of color. Persian rugs were strewn on the polished boards. There was no pretense at form or order. Icons hung next to the red-lacquered figures of Hindu gods. The curtains were nylon but the sofa cushions velvet. A white painted ladder lay flat under the ceiling, next to a skylight. A silk cord enabled the ladder to be pulled down to the floor. The man rising from the sofa had a high-bridged nose bursting from a moon-shaped face. His hair looked as if it had been poured from an oil bath. He was ten years older than the Canadian and wore tan trousers, brown-and-white shoes and a pink monogrammed shirt. His moist mouth showed good teeth.

"We'll speak English, I think that's best for you, no?" There was no hesitation at all. He used the language colloquially. He waited till his visitor was seated. "First tell me whether you are importing or exporting."

For all Macneil knew, the question was loaded, part of some cloak-and-dagger routine in which he was meant to provide the answer.

"Neither," he said flatly. "I write for a living."

Shashoua's face dissolved in a series of smiles. Each was a little narrower than its predecessor.

"A fascinating occupation. I envy you. No office, no telephone — just a piece of paper and a pencil."

"And something to say." Macneil lit a cigarette warily. Subterfuge was hardly his strong suit. "Let's not waste each other's time. Asher's dead."

The windows were shut tight. Air conditoners hummed in the uneasy silence. Shashoua picked his words with the delicacy of a dealer choosing diamonds.

"People who are supposed to be dead have a habit of

reappearing. That's why newspapers are particular about obituaries." He showed his teeth again.

"Not in this case," Macneil answered. "Half his chest was blown off."

Shashoua took the news without registering emotion. "I'm still not clear why you've come to me."

Macneil looked at the end of his cigarette. He made each gesture deliberate, milking the moment for impact.

"The last thing he tried to do was destroy your address, Mr. Shashoua. I did it for him. I think you'd better hear the rest of what I've got to say."

He told his tale for the second time that day. He might well have been talking into a recording machine. Shashoua listened, head bent. The hands holding his knees were almost effeminate in their delicacy. Macneil finished and looked up.

"I'll let you ask the questions."

Shashoua probed his ear gently. "You tell this Weber that you don't know Asher and then break jail with him. Didn't it occur to you this would be interpreted as a confession of guilt?"

"I saw what they did to your friend. I was next on the list."

Shashoua's voice was curious. "You weren't in the war?"

The Canadian shook his head. "I was seventeen years old when it finished. What's that got to do with it?"

"I was thinking aloud." The other man's shoulders rose and fell. "Tell me something — does Asher's death worry you?"

Macneil took a deep breath. "It could have been me. Would he have worried?"

"He might well have done. He worried about injustice."

"Did he now!" Macneil's tone was sarcastic. "Let me tell you what *I* think about you and your friend Asher. I think you're both in some dirty political power-play. I guess you'd call yourselves agents. Well get this straight. I wouldn't give a goddam if you were Stalin's uncle."

There was something levantine in the way Shashoua held his arms and shoulders. The elbows close to his ribs, the palms absolutely flat and sticking out.

"I'm a Jew," he said. "Asher was a Jew. Do you give a goddam about that?"

"Why *should* I?" Macneil answered deliberately. "Why is it that non-Jews are always supposed to spit or talk about 'some of their best friends'? All I know is that if it hadn't been for Asher, my wife wouldn't be where she is now. And as far as I'm concerned you *are* Asher."

Shashoua uncrossed his legs. He came out of his chair very slowly and walked across to the phone on the table. He looked back at Macneil. The Jew's eyes were suddenly formidable.

"Suppose I call the police. Suppose I tell them that I've never even heard of this Asher. They might feel inclined to keep you a little longer than you'd anticipated."

Macneil matched his calm menace. "A nice piece of drama but you won't use it. There's something you don't yet know. I told you, I was taking pictures when the men from P.I.D.E. stopped me. There was an hour-and-a-half gap between that and my arrest. The films were on their way out of the country by then. They arrived here on the plane from Montoro. I've got them."

Shashoua's hand crept from the phone. "Do you have them with you?"

"You're not even warm." Macneil shook his head, smiling. "I may be naive in this game but I'm not *that* naive. I'll tell you about them — three shots of a helicopter, taken at one thousandth of a second through a telescopic lens. The quality of the color is excellent. There are three men in the picture. The pilot, Weber and a friend."

A little mustache of sweat showed on Shashoua's upper lip. "Can you describe this third man?"

Macneil's hand described an easy arc. "I could if I thought it worth my while. I'll give you this much for free. He's tall — not as tall as Weber though — and in his sixties. He just could be a brewery salesman."

Shashoua was backing to the escritoire as he talked. "And what makes you think that I should be interested?" His hands went behind him.

"Because Asher was and Weber *is*." Macneil watched guardedly but Shashoua was holding nothing more than a roll of bills.

"You have a price, of course?" the Jew suggested.

Macneil's voice was bitter. "Sure I have a price. I just want the world put back forty-eight hours — to turn over in my bed and see my wife, asleep and happy. I want her to be able to bear our child in peace. But I'm learning fast — a guy has to be a realist. Maybe I'll have to settle for something less. Make me an offer!"

Shashoua was staring at the money on the table. He

spoke from a reverie that obviously moved him.

"My brother died in a factory for the extermination of Jews. He was privileged. He was gassed before being cremated. Asher's father died beside him."

A tiny hammer of excitement beat in Macneil's temple. The puzzle was taking shape but the key pieces were missing.

"That's bad but you've no right to involve me in your problems. I came here to talk about life, not death. *My* life — the lives of my wife and child."

Shashoua half-smiled, his mouth almost sad. "You've made that very clear. We're like you in one way, Mr. Macneil. We take care of our own. The difference is that we ask no outside help."

Macneil met his look fairly. The guy was an actor. There was no more compassion in his eyes than in Weber's. Both of them were ruthless bastards, indifferent to the means to achieve their ends.

"Don't you get me wrong, now," he warned. *"I'm* not asking you for help. I'm offering you a deal. Take it or leave it."

Shashoua wiped the sweat from his upper lip with a handkerchief. "I'd have to see the films first," he said carefully.

Another piece of the jigsaw dropped into place. Macneil waved dissent.

"No dice. It's got to be a straight swap. You've got friends. I want my wife delivered here in Puerto Vedra, unharmed."

"You can do that yourself," Shashoua said softly. His

face turned away. It was impossible to read his eyes. "Once I'm sure what is on those pictures, I could show you how."

"I wouldn't trust you, kneeling on a stack of Bibles," Macneil said, rising to his feet.

"Just one transparency," urged Shashoua. "You can keep the rest and the negatives. If you'll bring it here at three o'clock this afternoon, I'll give you the answer you want."

Macneil glanced around the room. There was no other door except the one leading to the stairway.

"Just the two of us, then," he warned. "Get rid of the woman."

Shashoua released his breath, a long drawn-out sound close to relief. He stood beside Macneil so that they both faced the long gilt mirror. His tone was ironical.

"Puzzle — which is the man of action? The one with the eyes like a cow and greasy hair or the tall one with the look of a Viking? It's the one with the greasy hair. You want Weber's head, I'll give it to you."

Macneil removed the hot hand from his shoulder. "It's not my day for whimsy. Three o'clock."

He hurried down the stairs and out to the street. A man behind detached himself from a doorway and followed. The hotel lobby was acrid with the stink of fly-kill. The desk clerk lowered his newspaper.

"The consulate called again. You've got to be there at nine in the morning."

It was the clerk's grin that really did it. Macneil leaned across the counter, his voice ominously low.

"Correction. They said would I *please* be there at nine in the morning, *right?*" His arm shot out, fingers gripping the clerk by the tie.

The man choked an apology. Macneil let him go. "If that call comes through, I'm across the square at Pinocchio's. Have them transfer it."

He hurried through a plate of pasta, washing it down with a glass of water. He'd drink no liquor till Pilar could drink with him. He passed the desk clerk without speaking and went up to his room. He took off his clothes and lay down on the bed. The big fan whirled slowly. The clamor of the phone brought him out of a doze. He struggled up, pushing his hand through hair damp with sweat.

"*Dígame!*"

The operator was nasally impersonal. "Your call to Ciudad de Montoro, señor. Go ahead, please."

Paláu's voice came and went in a crackle of static.

"It's me," Macneil said quickly. "Is it true about Pilar?"

"It's true, I'm afraid. There was nothing I could do. Everything we're saying is being monitored by the way. I saw General Zuimárraga this morning. One thing's sure. Her health will be taken care of. Are you listening, Dougal?" Paláu asked anxiously.

Macneil nodded as if the lawyer could see him. "Where is she?"

"San Vincente. I'm trying to get an order to see her. Nobody seems to want to give me one. They're all scared of Weber. If need be I'll go to the president. But don't expect a miracle."

"I wasn't counting on one," Macneil said in a tight voice. "If you get in, give her my love."

"And stay where you are," Paláu said urgently. "You understand what I mean."

"Adiós," said Macneil and hung up. His watch showed twenty-five to three. He showered quickly under a luke-warm needle spray. The box in the linen closet had not been disturbed. He took out a transparency and stuck the gun under his belt. It was already quarter to three when he went down. The desk clerk was laying out a hand of solitaire. The cigarette bobbed in his mouth as he counted the cards ostentatiously. He kept his eyes averted as the Canadian crossed the lobby. Macneil took another carriage to the Barrio Viejo. The narrow streets were less crowded, quieter. It was the hour of the siesta. People were catnapping in the bars, flies crawling in and out of their open mouths. Animals sought shade from the blinding sun.

He walked the last three hundred yards to the blue-painted house. The drunk had vanished. The short stretch of cobblestones was empty. He turned the door-knob, heart hammering a little. He wasn't sure what he expected but the back of his neck crawled with anticipation. The downstairs room was much as he had left it. There was no sign of the woman. A leaking faucet was dripping beyond the beaded curtain. He opened the door leading to the stairs. His nose reacted fractionally faster than his eyes or ears. It registered the smell of burned cordite as someone kicked the door shut. A hard object was rammed against the base of his spine. Fingers groped, locating the gun in his waistband. The man's mouth came close to Macneil's ear.

"*Hände hoch!*"

131

A jab from behind interpreted the words. He raised his arms slowly. The smell of explosion grew stronger as he climbed the stairs. The room was a shambles. Tables were upturned. The phone had been pulled out of the wall. Shashoua was lying by the escritoire, his glazed eyes searching the ceiling. His chin and chest were covered with blood from his open mouth. More blood dyed the Bokhara rug an even deeper red. It spread in a stream from a small hole in his forehead. He was no longer breathing.

Macneil was forced to turn away, sickened. He closed his eyes. A karate chop opened them for him. He spun around, his arms dropping helplessly. The force of the blow left his neck and shoulder muscles numbed. His assailant was a stringy individual in a flowered shirt that dangled outside his trousers. A center part divided his flat pale hair. Deep-set eyes considered Macneil coldly. The man switched his gun from left hand to right. His Spanish ripped like a buzz saw.

"The pockets — empty them onto the floor."

A pack of cigarettes fell, followed by a box of matches. A coin spun across the boards. Pain stabbed as Macneil's nerve centers registered returning feeling. He let the transparency fall last of all. The gunman's eyes flicked from the floor to Macneil. "Where are the others?"

"That's all there is," said Macneil. His gesture indicated the dead man. "I gave the rest to him."

The man's head moved from side to side like a snake's preparing to strike.

"You're lying! Where's the rest of them?"

It was the truth or a bullet in the skull. "In the hotel."

The man uncoiled. His thin mouth betrayed his satisfaction. He stepped over the fallen body to the window. He dragged the curtain aside and pulled it back again. It was obviously a signal. He jerked his head at Macneil.

"Put your things back in your pockets."

Macneil went down on one knee. His hands had started to shake. This was the end. The films wouldn't be enough for them. They'd butcher him as they'd butchered Shashoua. Six feet separated him from the man standing at the window. The gunman was watching the street. Macneil dove from a crouch. The German stepped sideways smartly, aiming the butt of the automatic at Macneil's head. The rug under his foot skidded on the polished boards. He fell heavily, his weapon thudding against the wall. They rolled together in a flurry of thrashing arms and legs. The bony knee that drove into Macneil's groin was no more than a couple of inches off target. He clutched desperately, sensing defeat once the holds got working. He rammed his head at the other man's face, butting like a goat. His forehead smashed against bone. Suddenly there was no more resistance. He climbed up shakily and leaned against the wall. The gunman was lying like a stunned steer, snuffling through a broken nose. The noise of a car outside galvanized Macneil to action. He looked down from the window. Two men were climbing out of a sand-colored station wagon. Fear touched him with a cold hand. He grabbed the gun from the floor and wrenched at the cord in the ceiling. The ladder descended easily. He heard the door open at the foot of the stairs as he went through the skylight. His wits sharpened with the instinct of self-preservation.

He was standing on a flat whitewashed roof in the shadow of the towering wall. The surrounding houses were all built alike, square and thick-walled with the same flat roofs. A water cistern gave him cover. He edged around it. A narrow passage ran at the back of the house. He went over the parapet and dropped. The landing jarred his aching body. A woman was emptying a chamber pot from a nearby balcony. He heard her shout of alarm as he sprinted down over the cobblestones. He ran through a network of lanes till exhaustion slowed him to a stumbling walk. He stopped in a doorway, legs gone, heart pumping. The wall was blessedly cool against his bruised forehead. He retched spasmodically till a voided stomach no longer responded. His back was clammy with effort. He forced himself into a trot again, shoving his way through the gathering crowds. His only hope was to reach the hotel before the gang of killers did. They must have known where he was from the start — followed him to Shashoua's place. They'd probably been wise to him from the moment he'd visited the photography store. *Fletcher,* he thought suddenly. Good old Charley Fletcher! And that meant P.I.D.E. Even here they operated and that clown at the consulate talked about surrender. He walked on, seeing Weber's eyes staring from the faces of strangers. A sense of anger and outrage weakened his fear. The bastards were no more than gangsters who made their own laws. Shashoua might be dead but he'd left a legacy behind.

The Jew's mealy voice sounded again, sly and confident. *You want Weber's head. I can give it to you.*

Macneil was beginning to think that he saw just how. He was still trotting when he reached the square. A green tourist bus was drawn up in front of the hotel. The lobby was crowded with Americans. A clamoring group blocked the desk clerk's view. Macneil ran upstairs. The doors along the corridor were open. The chambermaid was in a room, turning down the beds. He did his best to make his voice normal.

"Excuse me, señora. I forgot my key. Unlock my door, please."

She chose a key from a ring and let him in. He grabbed his bag and left it just inside the doorway. He could hear her moving about in the next room. He tiptoed to the end of the corridor. The transparencies were still in the shoe box. The chambermaid appeared as he left the storage room. He picked his bag up and walked by her quickly. He was halfway across the lobby when the clerk's head showed above the tourists.

"One moment, señor! Señor Macneil!"

Macneil hurried through the exit without looking back. A cab was unloading in front of a nearby bar. He climbed in on the blind side. A tan station wagon was crawling around the square toward the hotel.

"Police headquarters," said Macneil. He wondered why it sounded wrong.

"Si, señor." The driver took a hand off the wheel and rubbed the back of his neck expressively.

The station wagon gathered speed behind the taxi.

Macneil wedged himself in the corner. The big Chevrolet had come up close behind. The two men inside were wearing straw hats and sunglasses. Their faces were unrecognizable. The passenger slouched sideways, his hands hidden in his lap. Like a sniper waiting for the right moment and angle, Macneil thought, and turned his head away. He was out of his mind, going to the police. What did he have to offer except a threadbare story backed up by a wallet of color transparencies. That and the gun that had killed Shashoua. His own fingerprints were all over the weapon.

The cab was nearing the rotunda. Television and radio masts spiked the roof of what was called "Central America's most beautiful police headquarters." Once through those doors he was cold turkey.

"Never mind the police," he instructed. "Keep going."

The driver straightened out just at the last minute. The maneuver momentarily lost the station wagon. Macneil saw its nose behind a bus.

He leaned forward. "You want to earn twenty dollars?"

The hack answered over his shoulder. "Thirty."

Macneil grabbed the back of the seat. "You don't even know what I want you to do."

"I know," the man said calmly. "You want me to shake that station wagon that's been on our tail for the last ten minutes. Thirty."

Macneil dropped the bills into the driver's lap. The man's hand snaked them away. He glanced up at the driving mirror.

"They're as fast as we are. We'll have to do it another way. Leave it to me."

He had an air horn under the hood. He used it to blast his way through the traffic. He kicked down hard, ramming the accelerator at the floorboards.

"This ramp coming up — see it?"

Macneil nodded. The steep slope offered access to an overhead freeway. The road linked the city with the International Airport.

The driver gave his instructions. "I'll slow at the top. Have the door open, ready. As I make the turn, jump."

Macneil slid the catch back. The cars overhead were flicking by in rapid succession. There was no stopping on the freeway, no U-turns. The station wagon was only twenty yards behind now and uncovered.

"You're dead if the traffic cops catch you," the hack warned. "No pedestrians allowed. A big fine. Now!" He trod hard on the brake.

Macneil's legs were pumping as his feet hit the ground. He saw the door bang shut as the vehicle took the curve. The station wagon swung in. Its front end was coming straight at Macneil. He jumped up on the buffer strip, clinging to the top of the parapet. The Chevrolet hit the buffer with a crashing of headlamps. The car skated on, out of control. Macneil started running down the ramp. He had a brief vision of an alarmed face behind a windshield. The truck literally shaved him. He went over the parapet and dropped fifteen feet to the ground. The alley was crowded with garbage cans. He was somewhere in back of the Avenida Franco O'Farrell. It was a neighborhood of cheap bars and restaurants. The chase wouldn't end with the men in the station wagon. Others would be looking for him. He had to get off the streets.

He'd left his bag in the taxi. The odds against survival seemed suddenly very good. He hailed the first cab he saw and drove to the north end of the waterfront. He sat on the seawall, watching the vehicle turn and head back uptown. The waterfront came to an abrupt end. Board-walks over dirty yellow sand replaced the hardtop and mosaic pavements. The shoreline curved out to a light-house on the end of a mole. A fleet of small boats shel-tered in the stretch of shallow water. A network of gang-planks crisscrossed the mooring sites. He walked along slowly to a collection of ramshackle buildings. They all had false fronts made of clapboard. There were a couple of ships' chandler stores, a Chinese grocery and a bar called Ollie's. He picked his way over the sand to a shack that stood on its own. Hen-coop wire replaced the broken windows. There was a large Doberman lying at the foot of the door. Overhead was a sign.

MIKE DRURY   TARPON FISHING

The Doberman rose as Macneil came near. It bared its teeth in a soundless grimace. He shoved the door open. The paint-stained floor was littered with empty beer bottles. There was just enough room to move among the canvases that were drying on stretchers. Half a dozen fin-ished pictures featured the same subject matter — coun-try schoolhouse under a wintry sky. A boy was sledding down a slope, his scarf tails flying. Children bunched in a window of the school, watching him. The drawing was naive, the brushwork vigorous. The artist was sitting on a table, a palette in his hands. Shaggy blond hair topped a crumpled face. He was about forty and wore jeans and a very dirty T-shirt. He looked up, grinning greeting.

"Well if it isn't Hemingway himself! I thought you never moved out of Montoro these days — that beautiful wife of yours and all."

Macneil closed the door carefully. The huddle of sand-blown buildings was no-man's-land. Police patrols stopped at the end of the hardtop. Anything north of that line was likely to be connected with the smugglers. The *contrabandistas* policed their own community and gave the authorities no trouble.

"I need a boat, Mike," Macneil said quietly. "And I don't want to answer a whole lot of questions."

Drury slipped down from the table. He peered at the painting on the easel and stepped back, frowning.

"Do you think I'll ever get the goddam thing right?" he complained. "Here am I trying to show joy and envy and all the little bastards look as if they've peed themselves." He stepped over a pile of magazines. "I figured you might be in," he added casually.

Macneil's mouth opened. "You mean you *knew* I was in Puerto Vedra?"

Drury's head moved up and down. "You were seen."

Macneil took the news with misgiving. Drury wasn't the easiest guy in the world to handle. He'd turned up in Puerto Vedra seven years before. One hurried leap ahead of the Royal Canadian Mounted Police, gossip had it. Rumor or not, Drury had parlayed an iron nerve and a reputation for reliability into a profitable smuggling enterprise. Macneil had met him through Fletcher. Drury was often in Ciudad de Montoro.

There was a newspaper lying open on the desk. The caption drew him like a magnet.

MONTORAN MINISTER GIVES COUNTRY CLEAN BILL OF HEALTH

His Excellency General Ilidio Zuimárraga flew in from Panama yesterday on his way home. Interviewed at the International Airport, General Zuimárraga repeated the statement he made at the recent meeting of security chiefs in Panama City. Montoro, he said, had no security problem. The recent wave of student unrest had left his country unmarked. What was left of a once-powerful right-wing movement was totally discredited. Infiltration by Castro agents was unknown. The general said he was conscious of a new spirit abroad throughout Central America. It was a combination of our Catholic heritage, enlightened thinking and plain common sense. The general, a onetime director of P.I.D.E., left for the sister-republic in a jet chartered from Puerto Vedran Airways.

The picture in the box showed a fat man staring into the camera wearily, as if he'd done it all before, too often. Macneil ripped out the page, folded it in four and put it in his pocket.

"I've got to get home," he said simply. "I don't have a passport and I'm in trouble with the law."

Drury's tongue followed the movements of his paintbrush. He added a blob of brown to the schoolhouse roof.

"You're putting me on. How could a guy like you be in trouble with the law?"

"Ask P.I.D.E.," said Macneil. "That's not everything. They've got Pilar inside. This is a straightforward proposition, Mike. I'll give you five hundred bucks to land me in Montoro. I don't have that much with me but you'll get it."

The Doberman was whining at the door. Drury threw a book at the wall and the whining stopped. His eyes were shrewd.

"Is Charley Fletcher involved in this?"

Macneil rubbed the back of his neck. The karate chop still pained him.

"Yes. Just how much I don't know as yet."

Drury's face creased into a sour grin. "Strike one against you. That old blabbermouth's had it coming for years. All the times I've told him, 'Charley' I'd say, 'you and I could make a fortune together using the travel agency.' All he did was holler like a goosed duchess. And what happens, he teams up with an amateur!"

"It's not like that. It's not like that at all," said Macneil.

"Well, what *is* it like?" demanded Drury.

Macneil shook his head. "I can't go into it, Mike. The main thing is that I need your help."

Drury's hand swung up in protest. "Now wait a minute — let's get a couple of things straight first. We're both Canadians but nobody's running the flag up! You and I have played some poker together. Your wife's a nice girl. That's as far as it goes."

Macneil slipped the gun out of his pocket. "I'm sorry, Mike. Pilar's having a baby in four weeks' time."

Drury pursed his lips and whistled. "Put that thing away before someone gets clobbered." He pointed through the window. "See those boats out there. One of them is *my*

141

baby. I've got forty thousand dollars tied up in her. You're offering me five hundred to make a trip that could end in my losing her. Does that make sense?"

"I'll double it," Macneil said desperately.

"Not a chance." Drury's glance was curious. "When a guy like you does go wrong he usually finishes hotter than pan fat. I don't want to wind up in the cell next to you, knocking on the wall for company."

Macneil put the gun back in his pocket. It would never have worked and they both knew it. He went on doggedly.

"I went to the consulate this morning. Pollard wants me to surrender to the police here."

Drury blew with disgust. "What else did you expect? He's been trying to get his hands on my passport ever since I came here. So?"

"Another man's died since then."

"Another . . . hold it!" A look of extreme pain spread over the other man's face. "Don't say another word — I'm a Baptist in good standing. Just tell me one thing. Can you handle a boat?"

The suggestion revived all Macneil's hopes. He answered eagerly. "My father always had boats. I can handle most."

Drury leaned on the windowsill. The hair on his tanned forearms was the color of the bleached woodwork.

"See that black cruiser — the one to the right of the washing — she's the *Rosa Negra*. There's fuel aboard and there's water. I know where the keys are. She belongs to a creep called Voss."

The black hull bobbed apart from its neighbors, distinctive in the fleet of lighter-colored craft. Macneil backed away from the window. His voice was apprehensive.

"What am I supposed to do, steal it?"

Drury picked the paint from his fingernails. The way in which he let his breath go was a measure of his impatience.

"Is 'stealing' a bad word in your book? Look, I'm trying to get you off the hook, friend. You'd better make your mind up."

"For crissakes," Macneil said hastily. "I'm just wondering what sort of a chance I'd have. I'm not so sure about the navigation part. It's been a long time."

"Bullshit," said Drury. "You've got about eighty miles to Ciudad de Montoro on a straight course. That boat'll make it in seven hours. There's a tide just after ten. I'm going out myself. You can tag on behind as far as the roadstead."

He fished a couple of bottles from the icebox and knocked the caps off. Macneil's teetotal resolutions were forgotten. He drank the cold beer gratefully. Use the small pleasures while you could. He put the empty bottle on the floor.

"I guess that's it, then. A guy like me can't expect much more."

Drury belched. "I don't understand you any too well, Mac. You seem to think you're entitled to more than you're getting. What would *you* do in my place?"

Macneil's shoulders rose and fell. "Probably nothing," he said with honesty. "Anyway I've finally taken a long

look at myself. Alone means that you do it yourself —
everything. How do I get the keys?"

"You ask for them." Drury's eyes were still curious. He
seemed on the point of saying something and thought better of it. "They're in a locker in the Chinaman's store.
Voss keeps a few things there. I don't even know why he
moors this end of the waterfront. Except that he's a blow-
hard. Maybe he likes to impress his friends. Mixing with
the rascals. He's in Guatema City over the week-end
anyway. The Chinaman won't ask questions. Where are
you going to head for?"

The island was clear in Macneil's memory — a fifty-acre
clump of pine and eucalyptus in the river near Paláu's
home.

"The Rio Verde estuary."

Drury kicked his way through the litter to a shelf. He
took down a chart and dusted it off. He spread a sheet of
art paper out on the table and sketched in the coastline
with a felt pen. He plotted a course from north to south
and looked at it admiringly.

"That ought to be worth something, even unsigned."

Macneil groped in his pocket. Drury caught his sleeve.
"Put it away. That's not what I meant. All my life I've
been doing the wrong thing. Maybe I'm right for once. I
told you, your wife's a nice girl." He bent over the homemade chart. "Noboby will bother you while you're in
Puerto Vedran waters. Your trouble might start about
here. The Montorans have a couple of MTB's with sonar
equipment. Your bet's to go in with the fishing fleet. You
ought to catch up with them around sunup." He rolled the
stiff paper and snapped an elastic band around it.

"What happens to the boat afterward?"

Drury's gesture signified disinterest. "Knock a hole in her. I told you, Voss is a creep."

"Thanks, Mike," Macneil said awkwardly. "I'll remember this if I make it."

Drury sucked on a tooth. "You'll make it. You can't afford not to. You'd better get aboard as soon as you can. Check the motor. You'll see my riding lights any time after ten. And remember, your arse is in a crack — watch yourself." He opened the door and winked as Macneil went out.

A ring of coconut palms sheltered the small frame store. Macneil trudged across the hot yielding sand and entered a cool darkness smelling of dried fish and spice. A very old Chinese crept into the one patch of sunlight in the store. He stood there blinking and smiling.

"Voss sent me for the keys, Uncle," Macneil said easily. "OK?"

The old man shuffled away, most of his patter incomprehensible. "All time hurry, Uncle, hurry! Not thinking about rainy season, rats coming. You want stores?"

Macneil went after him. "Just a few things, Uncle." The locker was a hinged tea chest. He lifted the lid. There was a pair of binoculars at the bottom of the chest. A set of keys was tied to the leather strap. He lifted out the glasses. The lens were bloomed and calibrated, expressly designed for night work. He slung the binoculars around his neck. The old man filled a carton with bread, ham and fruit. He added a dozen cans of beer and made change. His rheumy eyes were anxious.

"You fellows going fishing, maybe. Catch squid, don't

throw away. Uncle like." He rubbed his belly, grimacing.

"I'll remember," said Macneil. He carried the groceries back to the seawall. Drury's shack was deserted. The Doberman had gone. The noise and activity were concentrated in Ollie's Bar. He heard an Australian voice loud with accusation. A wooden landing stage was chained to the blocks of stone. He lowered himself down. The catwalks seemed to have been laid haphazardly. They were no more than flimsy lengths of boards zigzagging from one craft to another. He made his precarious way to the black boat. A red-faced man in shorts was sitting under a square of sailcloth. He held his place in his book as Macneil stepped on and off his deck. He spat over the side expressively and returned his attention to his book. A rope handrail helped Macneil to the thirty-foot cabin cruiser. He unlocked the wheelhouse. The timber was teak. A perspex shell covered the cockpit. A cantilever arrangement enabled the cover to be swung back at will. He lifted the engine hatch. The Mercedes diesel was capable of fifteen knots, with the needle on the rev counter well below the red line. He closed the hatch and let fresh air into the cockpit. It was past eleven but the setting sun still had strength. There was one small instrument panel, a single-level control. The wheel spun lazily as the cruiser lifted on the faint swell.

He took the carton of groceries below. A short ladder led directly into the saloon. There was nothing there but bench seats and a table bolted to the floor. The aft cabin had two bunks. A pair of nylons draped the brass casing of the porthole. There were some trashy paperbacks on the bunk and a book on navigation. He left his jacket there and went forward. The galley had an icebox and gas cooker. Next to it was a combined lavatory and shower. He checked the fuel and water tanks. The gauges showed that both were full.

He primed the diesel and hit the starting button. The motor ground on uselessly for a minute and then caught fire. *Rosa Negra*'s hull shuddered. He looked back at the shore and cut the motor. None of the nearby craft showed signs of life. A strong rope attached to a mooring post sunk in cement held *Rosa Negra* by the stern. A drag anchor stopped her bow from swinging around. The channel ahead was thirty yards wide. All he had to do was point the cruiser at the oil tankers lying in the channel and open the throttle. Drury's boat was moored a hundred feet away. A radio mast with two crosspieces identified it clearly. Macneil closed the cockpit and locked the wheelhouse on the inside. He went below again and stretched out on a bunk. It was the first time he'd ever really looked at the gun that had killed Shashoua. It was a Belgian-made .32, its long barrel weighted by a heavy butt. He released the clip. Only one shot had been fired. He replaced the magazine and pumped a shell into the breech. God knows what memory prompted that bit of expertise. Maybe he should be doing this sort of thing for a living. Death no longer seemed to trouble him too much. He put the gun under the pillow and took the transparencies from his jacket pocket. The pictures of the group in front of the helicopter fascinated him. The third man was obviously a German. He looked it and Shashoua had hinted as much.

So what — any country south of Mexico was full of them. And yet Shashoua had equated this particular man with Weber's defeat. Why?

A rumbling in his stomach reminded him that he'd eaten twice in thirty-six hours. He cut himself a truck driver's sandwich and drank a can of beer. He was strangely confident. Part of it came from Drury. There had been a tacit admission that he'd make the eighty miles in safety. Any doubt Drury had seemed centered on what came afterward. Macneil lay back, putting his hands behind his head. He knew instinctively what Weber expected of him. The colonel would be sure that he held the stronger cards. Fair enough but if it was poker they were playing, a strong steady bluff could take the pot with a pair of deuces.

Darkness came suddenly. A faint breeze set the surrounding boats bobbing and rolling. The shoreline had turned into a sweep of jumping glittering lights. He went aloft and stood staring across at Drury's boat. A pair of colored lamps hung on the radio mast. At twenty past ten Drury started his motor. Macneil hit his own starter. He worked feverishly, casting off and hauling up the drag anchor. The cruiser swung around, pitching as she felt the drag of the tide. He took the wheel and gave the motor throttle. By the time they reached open water Drury's boat was twenty yards ahead. The stars were already out, pinpricks of light in a velvet dome. The moon flooded the sea with silver. He rolled with the movement of the boat, the wash from Drury's boat blowing back in his face.

WERNER WEBER

THE PREMISES of the Gavilan Trading Company were in a downtown building owned by the Christian Brothers. An illuminated cross topped the narrow eighteen-story structure. Small craft making for the *Presidente* section of the city frequently steered by the cross. It was a frame of reference that left Weber unmoved. He used an entrance at the back and went up the service stairs. The maneuver was as much for Rittberg's sake as for his own. Every building superintendent in Ciudad de Montoro turned in a weekly report to P.I.D.E. — after-hour callers, any unusual activity. Ironically enough, Rittberg's name had already shown up on Weber's desk a couple of times in the past. The windows were open at the end of the seventh-floor corridor. Weber paused to get his breath. Hot sunshine searched the polished linoleum. A metal plate shone on a nearby door.

GAVILAN TRADING COMPANIA S.A.   HELMUT RITTBERG

There was only one office, a large room overlooking the port. Shipping-line posters brightened the walls. There was some functional furniture and a Telex machine on a stand. Weber shut the door and turned the key. The man

149

in the chair by the window leaned back, looking at Weber out of pouched eyes. He was a worn forty with a dissatisfied mouth and a damp shirt showing the mat of hair beneath. He nodded at the Telex stand.

"It's timed ten-o-seven but they'd been trying since nine."

Weber picked up the message. It was in plain and by-lined Puerto Vedra. He read it through three times and ripped it to pieces. He dropped the torn bits into the trash basket.

"They've killed the Jew."

Rittberg shrugged. "You gave the assignment to Dudek. You ought to have known."

Weber turned his back on him, looking out through the window. For people like Rittberg, the movement had become a sort of club where they drank beer and remembered the Schwarzwald under rain. Violence for them had become vicarious. Meanwhile Shashoua was dead and the Canadian was on the run again. He spoke with authority.

"Send this message to El Salvador. Quote, 'Stand by for emergency instructions over agreed route' unquote. You can sign it Schulze."

Rittberg made a long arm and scribbled the words on a pad. "I'll get it off immediately."

Weber checked the time. He was ten minutes late already. His appointment was for eleven.

"Stay away from that machine once you've got the message off," he ordered. He unlocked the door, making sure that the corridor was empty. He used the service stairs again, leaving the building by another exit. He parked under the plane trees in the courtyard. Zuimárraga's car was behind the fountain. The duty officer hurried across as Weber climbed out of the Mercedes.

"The general's in your office, Colonel."

Weber flexed his shoulders, his eyes on the matron's quarters. "Kokoscka?"

The duty officer shook his head. "He hasn't left, Colonel. He slept here."

Weber slung his jacket over his shoulder, sweat trickling down his ribs.

"How many men have you got watching my quarters — my apartment, I mean?"

The duty officer's eyes were puzzled. "The orders are standard, sir. One during the day, two at night."

"Call them off," said Weber. "There's to be no watch on my place till further orders."

He strode over the grass, the heat rising in waves. He was conscious of the woman standing at the window on his right. Zuimárraga's attempt to see her the previous night might have stemmed from no more than curiosity. But it was no time to take chances. Zuimárraga was sitting in Weber's chair behind the desk, unexpectedly elegant in a white linen suit and black silk tie. He turned his mournful face on Weber, his dewlaps shaking.

"Forgive me for using your chair, Colonel. I prefer not to have that woman staring at me. This whole thing is becoming a headache. Paláu has asked for a presidential audience. The secretariat refused and referred him back to me. But the man's influential. I can't hold him off indefinitely."

Weber pulled a corner of the curtain, screening most of the room from the woman at the window. There was something very soft about Zuimárraga, an instability of character typical of Latin Americans.

"I'm aware of that, sir," he said calmly. "I told you on the phone last night. We know that Macneil's been to the Canadian consulate. It's probable that they've issued him with some sort of travel document. The frontier posts are on the lookout but he's not likely to announce his arrival."

The general settled his hands on his belly. "You seem very sure that he *will* be coming back."

"Quite sure, sir." Weber smiled thinly. "I think you are too. There are fifty ways he can enter the country undetected. This doesn't worry me. I know where he'll head for."

Zuimárraga found his scalp with a fat finger. He scratched delicately as though fearful of disturbing his hair arrangement.

"You do?" he asked sardonically. "You're not expecting him to walk in *here* by any chance?"

Weber lit one of his cheroots. He blew a stream of smoke, moving his head from side to side.

"Then where?" probed the general. "The man doesn't sound like a fool. He won't go to the lawyer's house, let alone his own place."

Weber had no intentions of sharing his inner conviction. "I think the less you know about it at this stage the better, General. Macneil thinks he has business here. I intend to see that it's *unfinished* business."

Zuimárraga sat up straight, looking like a worried

bloodhound. "You realize the position I'll be in if I have to go to the president about this?"

"I realize the position we'll *both* be in," Weber answered. "Rest assured, General, it won't come to that. There'll be no trial, no scandal." He closed his hand on a cloud of smoke and opened his fingers. "No more than that," he added significantly.

Zuimárraga struggled out of his chair. "You have till Monday, Colonel. I can hold off Paláu that long. You'll have to give me something definite at the end of it though. He'll take a lot of discouraging."

Each man gauged the other's silence. Weber mashed his cigarette with a sudden movement.

"You have my word on it."

Zuimárraga was blowing with the effort of leaving his chair. "I suppose this assurance of yours is contagious. I've noted it in your men. You know, there's an odd feeling about coming to San Vincente — it's almost like being a trespasser."

"If you're talking about last night," Weber put in quickly, "Kokoscka's orders were specific. *No one* is allowed access to Señora Macneil. I'd have thought the reasons would be obvious. If I'd known you wanted to visit her . . ."

The General's hand dismissed the suggestion. "I realized I was wrong at the time, Weber. I may have criticized your methods sometimes but I've never tried to interfere with you. I'll be at the ministry if you want me."

Weber pulled the curtain back again. He watched Zuimárraga as far as he could before speaking into the intercom box.

"Moreno? Now listen carefully. I want a round-the-clock watch on Paláu and Fletcher — a *discreet* watch — choose the right men. They'll report to you personally."

He opened the door to the cloisters. The face at the window had gone. Zuimárraga's car was no longer in the courtyard. Weber called the duty officer out of the guard-house.

"If there are any inquiries about the prisoner, you'll say that she's no longer here. Is that clear?"

The duty officer nodded understanding. "There was a call only a few minutes ago, Colonel. I took it myself."

The sunshine was hot on Weber's head. "A foreigner?"

The duty officer's eyes widened. "The colonel already knows?"

Weber towered over him. "I gave orders for *all* these calls to be traced. Where did this one come from?"

The man answered anxiously. "I have the slip inside, sir. Captain Moreno left instructions that the details would be collected by his office."

Weber broke in impatiently. "Never mind Moreno's instructions."

The duty officer blinked. "The call was traced to the Fortuna Bar. It's on the embarcadero, near the bullring."

Precisely where the car had been stolen from. Macneil seemed to like the neighborhood. Weber's mouth dragged into a hard smile.

"Don't bother, I'll tell *you* what happened. This man gave no name. All he asked was if Señora Macneil was in custody. You said you had no authority to pass out this kind of information, right?"

The P.I.D.E. man moved his eyes cautiously. "Yes, sir."

Weber widened his smile. "So you flashed a signal to the communications room. The next time you spoke, the phone was dead."

The man swallowed hard. "I'm sorry, sir," he said awkwardly. "That's exactly the way it was. In fact, I heard him replace the receiver."

Weber nodded affably. "He'll call again. This time you can tell him what he wants to know. Say that Señora Macneil was here but she has been removed for further questioning. You don't know where."

He drove downtown and parked behind the bullring. The open stretch between there and the two markets was snarled with traffic. Irate cops moved among the throng, blowing their whistles, cuffing the odd urchin stealing from the fruit vendors. The bay was bright with the colored sails of the anchored fishing fleet. He leaned on the wheel, staring at the bar on the far side. A striped awning extended over a small terrace. Behind the waterfront facade was a warren of bulging-fronted houses connected by narrow passages. Tiny squares were wedged between top-heavy buildings. Garbage decomposed in the tropical heat. The whitewashed walls were streaked with ammonia. Every other doorway led to a bar. The night finished at daybreak, marimba-players drinking coffee with the last whore on duty. Machete murders were common. Thieves went to ground in the sewer tunnels. The whole area was a headache to the criminal police. If Macneil had gone to ground there, he'd picked his place wisely. There was no doubt in Weber's mind that the Canadian was back in

Montoro. The scene was almost set, no more than the last pieces remained to be shifted.

He lifted the radiophone and asked for the guardroom. "Weber. No calls are to be made to this number till further orders. Refer all business to Captain Moreno."

He backed out of the parking lot and filtered into the northbound lane. Workmen were erecting stands on each side of the Avenida de Libertad. Chairs had been placed on every inch of space between the grass shoulder and the fountains. Scaffolding stretched from the waterfront to the presidential palace. The Mercedes crawled forward, the sound of its horn lost in the general fanfare. He had almost forgotten the chaos of the hours that were to come. The interminable processions of hooded *penitentes* winding through packed crowds to the accompaniment of drumbeats. There'd be the racket of two hundred church bells tolling. The streets would be filled with priests and nuns. And on the last stroke of the bell carnival would erupt!

The roads into the city were heavy with traffic. Overloaded buses, field hands crammed into open trucks. Indians trudged along behind their burros in a cloud of dust. The Presidential Causeway was a shimmering strip of black across the vivid green of the rice paddies. It was cooler once the grades grew steeper. The forest of mountain pines lay silent in the setting sun. He drove through the gates, past the giant cedars and onto the tanbark. He wiped his face and hands on a handkerchief sprinkled with cologne. He slammed the car door and ran up the steps. There were no servants anywhere. Von Ostdorf's voice called him from the study. He was sitting with his back to the open window, still wearing his leather breeches. This time stockings and matching sweater were a pale shade of lemon.

"Your message said an hour." His tone was reproving.

Weber's eyes missed nothing. The small safe was shut but ashes smoldered in the fire grate. The scene reminded him of another evening, twenty-four years ago.

Von Ostdorf seemed to read his mind. "So many papers — one gets forgetful. What's the trouble?"

The mannered nonchalance was difficult to assess. "The Jews have been here," Weber said tersely.

Von Ostdorf's cheeks turned a perceptible shade paler. "The *Jews!*"

Weber nodded. "What I'm telling you is strictly between us. What happened could have been disastrous. As it is, I think we're in the clear. The next forty-eight hours will show one way or another. Our immediate problem is Schulze."

Von Ostdorf looked a shaken man. "I'm entitled to know something more than that," he protested.

Weber towered above him. "You're entitled to know whatever I tell you. This might mean a change in our plans. A return to Salvador."

Von Ostdorf ran his fingers the length of his monocle cord. "Does that mean you've alerted them too?"

Weber nodded. "If it comes to the worst, Montoro's going to be no place for a man in my position."

The baron massaged his scraggy neck. "What role did you have in mind for me?"

Weber looked down at him. "There's only room for the pilot and two passengers. I go with Schulze. Otto can fend for himself."

The baron took his hand away from his throat. "He and I are expendable, is that it?"

Weber spread his legs, making every word tell. "I'll repeat what I said before. I still think we're in the clear, but I've been too long in this business. When I'm sure I'm never certain. I'm the one who'll be in danger, not you. You can always run to your numbered account in Zurich. To each his own, as they say."

Von Ostdorf came to his feet, displaying his well-preserved teeth. "There are times when I wish we'd been friends, Weber. You're still able to astonish me with observations like that. 'To each his own.' It's almost philosophical. And just how much of all this do you intend telling our guest?"

Weber's big shoulders filled his jacket. "You can hear for yourself. Meanwhile you and I can be quite sure about each others' interests."

A peacock screamed in the shadows under the cedars. Von Ostdorf listened till the echo had died. "Quite clear," he said quietly. "Shall we go?"

Weber followed him into the hall. The women's voices sounded in the kitchen quarters. The baron led the way down to the cellars. The whitewashed walls were bright in the sudden light. They walked through the arches to the massive steel door. Von Ostdorf touched a bell and positioned himself next to Weber. Both men faced the concealed television camera. The outer door started moving back on the rollers. They hurried down the passage,

Weber in front with his head bent. He was certain of one thing. If his plan failed, he could save himself from a firing squad but never from Von Ostdorf's enmity. As long as they both lived, the baron would be seeking to destroy him.

He pushed the door leading to the living quarters. The air was strong with the smell of liquor. Otto had drawn himself up, heels together, shoulders square. His tan was yellow in the artificial light. The man sitting on the lower bunk was naked from the waist up. His belt suspended two flabby rolls of flesh. His bullet head swung from one visitor to the other.

Weber clicked to attention. "Baron von Ostdorf, sir."

Dark pads hung under Schulze's eyes. He kicked a glass over as he rose, extending his hand.

"So! After all these years, Baron. I regret that we never met in former times."

Von Ostdorf's smile was courtly. "My apologies for a very poor hospitality, sir."

Weber jerked his head at the door. "Wait outside till you're called, Otto."

The blond youngster stepped smartly to the passage. Weber righted the empty glass and turned.

"Bad news, I regret, sir. There's a possible change of plan. You might have to go back to Salvador."

Schulze glowered suspiciously. "On whose orders — what happened?"

Weber's answer was careful. "Something that never could have been foreseen. I thought it best to inform you. Baron von Ostdorf agrees."

Von Ostdorf turned his head, his monocle catching the

light. He looked like the guest of honor at some testimonial dinner — modest in face of fulsome praise.

"My opinion was pure formality, sir. Colonel Weber can always be trusted to make the right decisions."

The undercurrent of sarcasm was not lost on Weber. He eyed the unmade bed, hiding his distaste. The man had made a pigsty of the place in twenty-four hours. Schulze scratched at the matted gray hair on his chest.

"I don't give a shit about all that! What I want to know is what has happened."

Von Ostdorf broke in before Weber could answer. "It appears that the colonel has uncovered a plot, sir. There are Jewish agents in Montoro."

Schulze leaned forward, clutching at his chest. His breathing was suddenly irregular. Weber's features masked a cold rage. Von Ostdorf's attack had been totally unpredicted — a live hand grenade thrown without warning.

Schulze's voice rose to a near scream. *"Jewish agents?* I demand an explanation, Colonel!"

Weber stared back stonily. "Baron von Ostdorf has his tenses wrong, sir. It's true that two men have been traced here but both have been liquidated."

"Treachery!" bellowed Schulze. "Ever since I left Chile, I've been surrounded by traitors and incompetents! Why do these Jews choose me as a scapegoat! How is it that my movements are known to my enemies!" He lumbered across to the wall and stood with his back to it. He stretched his arms wide, his mouth spraying spittle. "Crucify me and be done with it!"

Weber hurried over. Schulze shook him off, ranting on

till lack of breath brought his tirade to an end. He dropped onto the bunk and buried his head in his hands. He looked up again, glowering.

"Let me remind you that I still give the orders, Colonel. I want to get out of this place as soon as possible. Make the necessary arrangements."

Weber shifted his weight from one leg to the other. The picture flickered on one of the television screens. The last of the sun gilded the clearing in the pine forest.

"We can't afford to be premature, sir. It's taken four months to arrange your escape route. Many people are involved. Returning to Salvador unless it's essential could endanger their lives and liberty."

"Then what the hell is this all about?" Schulze shouted. "Why have you come here?"

"To explain my position," Weber said doggedly. "What has happened can only affect me. Nothing can endanger *your* safety. You have my word for this."

He was sick of the scene, ashamed for the man he was looking at. Schulze struggled into his shirt. He buttoned it slowly, his eyes cunning.

"What do you think, Von Ostdorf?"

The baron's smile held a hint of ruefulness. "I'm afraid I'm not entirely in the colonel's confidence. Nevertheless I respect his judgment."

Schulze poured a glass of brandy. He drank it greedily and wiped his mouth on the back of his hand.

"My life's in your hands," he proclaimed dramatically. "I can do no more than I've done for the cause."

Weber turned his wrist. It was already well past four. "I've given you my assurance, sir. You have the radio —

161

you'll be kept informed. I think you and I had better go, Baron. There's a lot to be done." He looked across at Von Ostdorf.

The baron's voice was smoothly regretful. "I'm not much help. Like Herr Schulze, all I can do is wait."

Schulze beat his fists on his knees, his voice near a scream again. "I'm a sick man — I can't stand this uncertainty. Now for God's sake *do* something! I'm relying on you, Weber."

Weber brought his heels together. It was clear that Von Ostdorf had no intention of leaving the bunker.

"At your orders, sir." The baron accompanied him to the door. Otto was standing a dozen feet along the passage. The baron smiled slyly.

"Colonel Weber's leaving, Otto. Let him out."

The blond youngster flattened himself against the wall. Weber pushed past without a word. The massive steel door rumbled shut behind him, the noise reverberating through the cellars.

He reached the city shortly after five. Bands of *penitentes* were gathering outside the churches. Some of them were barefooted, others carried homemade scourges and chains. All wore the hooded gowns. Each parish had its effigy or relic to be borne through the streets, followed by a parade of small girls with wet knickers carrying bouquets. He narrowed his nostrils fastidiously. The streets seemed to have stored the earlier heat. The occasional breeze was even more torrid. His muscles and nerves had been fighting the tropical summers for too long now. It was not age but the feeling of suffocation that was slowing his reflexes.

162

He left the Mercedes in the forecourt. Numbers stenciled on the concrete identified his parking space. He looked across at the terra-cotta building. The security guards were usually hanging around near the main entrance. He called headquarters on the radiophone.

"I'm going off the air in a couple of minutes. What news do you have?"

Moreno answered doubtfully. "There's nothing much, sir. Fletcher hasn't left his apartment all day. The girl's alone in the travel agency. I've got two good men tailing the lawyer."

"Keep after them both — Fletcher as well as Paláu. How about Kokoscka?"

A hint of embarrassment crept into the other man's voice. "The woman's refusing to eat, sir."

Weber frowned. "Keep bringing the food. I'll call you later." He replaced the receiver. Prickly heat seemed to burst from every pore in his body. He thought of the coming bath, needles of cold water blasting the sweat from his skin. The business at the bunker still troubled him. Von Ostdorf had to be very sure of himself. He'd made his first move with almost open contempt. Weber took the long-barreled Luger from the glove compartment. He slipped it under the front passenger seat. Anyone leaving the car would present his back to the driver. A tilt of the seat . . . He locked the Mercedes and walked across the forecourt. A smell of burned rubber hung in the lobby. The tubbed plants were littered with cigarette ends and burned matches. The half-caste janitor was repairing a hole in a plaster pillar. Weber thumbed the button for the express elevator.

163

"Someone might be asking for me, Francisco. You needn't say that I mentioned it but he's all right."

The janitor smoothed the compound with his trowel. He stepped back and nodded satisfaction.

"Your men have gone, Colonel. You know that?"

The cage door slid open. "I know," said Weber. "This friend I'm expecting — he hasn't been here before and I know you're careful about strangers."

The janitor picked up his ladder. "I won't be here much longer. The processions start at seven."

Weber touched the button. The worn elevator rattled its way up to the penthouse floor. He let himself into his apartment and leaned against the door. The elevator shaft was twenty feet along the corridor. His ear recognized every tremor of the system, the final crash that announced its arrival. Macneil's alternative was an approach by the service stairs. An arduous climb to a fireproof door and the roof.

Weber went out onto his terrace. The tubbed bushes and trelliswork separated it from those of his neighbors. The heat was still unbearable. He walked as far as the parapet and peered over. The first lines of marchers were winding down the hilly streets behind the apartment building. He could hear the beating of the drums, an ominous tattoo that carried plainly. He went inside again. No matter which approach Macneil chose there would be ample warning. He arranged the big room carefully. The chair with its back to the terrace if the Canadian came through the french windows. Another chair at the desk if he came through the front door. Weber tried each position, his broad shoulders a target for an assailant outside. He ran no risk. Macneil's visit would be designed as the prelude to his wife's release. And for that he needed the colonel.

Weber unlocked a drawer in his desk. He loaded two more guns and scotch-taped one to the underside of each chair. He wasn't going to make his move till Macneil was safely inside the apartment. He rested for a while then showered and changed his clothes. The sun had set. The tropical fish in the tank glimmered phosphorescently. The sudden ringing of the outside phone startled him. He picked up the handset.

"Weber."

The voice was familiar. "Paragon Laundry."

Weber's fingers tightened. The code greeting identified Rittberg. It was at the same time a warning and only used in time of emergency. His answer was guarded.

"Go ahead but make it short."

"A message from Salvador. The shipment has been cleared for Puerto Vedra. The helicopter's on its way."

"Thank you," Weber said carefully. He hung up. The room seemed to have gone much darker. A neon sign on a neighboring roof reached in across his ceiling. He wiped his mouth, the gesture curiously studied — as if he needed to assure himself of self-control.

He used the red phone this time, his voice dull with the certainty of impending disaster. His demand sparked a flurry of action. The connection he wanted was made within seconds. The frontier post he was calling was high in the Sierra Araña. Von Ostdorf's plantation was no more than thirty kilometers away over rough mountain roads.

He put the question calmly, knowing the answer already. "Have you had a party of three men through recently — two Chileans and a Montorese?"

The man's reply was immediate. "An hour ago, Colonel. They were traveling in a B.M.W. sedan. They're the only ones we've had through all day as it happens. No trouble, I hope — their papers were in order."

"No trouble," said Weber. The microphone clattered from his hand. *Von Ostdorf's car.* He must have applied the pressure the moment he had left. Persuading his guest would have been no problem. Otto was just makeweight. Once over the border into Puerto Vedra they'd be airborne within minutes. It was too late to do anything about it.

He moved in the darkness like a sleepwalker. He found a bottle and glass, poured himself a double shot of rum. He stood by the window, his thoughts shaping and dissolving like patterns in a kaleidoscope. Von Ostdorf was gambling on his failure to deal with the situation. The move would establish the baron as the man of lightning decision, his guest's savior. It left Weber holding the bag. A candidate for the firing squad or an incompetent fool scrambling out of a dilemma that should never have been in the first place. Either dead or discredited.

He poured himself another drink. This time he added ice and lime juice. He unlatched the front door and left it ajar. He lit a cheroot and sat down facing the french windows. It was quarter-past ten. There was nothing to do now but wait.

DOUGAL MACNEIL

THE WHEEL was like a live thing in his hands. The last of the night trailed off in pink tassels. A crescent of fire rose on the horizon. The coastline to the west was a hazy blur. The following breeze still held, ruffling the water ahead. The course Drury had plotted had taken the cruiser south of the reefed atolls that the smugglers used as dumps. It was just after five A.M. He glanced down at the chart. Drury had penciled in estimated times and distances. He was dead on schedule. Another hour would bring him to the mouth of the Rio Verde. He clamped the wheel and cut his speed to ten knots an hour. The motor had been running for hours on full throttle but showed no sign of overheating.

The bow lifted rhythmically, sending a fine spray pluming over him. He was half-naked in the rising sun, wearing no more than his shorts. He went below and made coffee. He took his breakfast up to the cockpit. He ate the rough sandwiches like a man uncertain of his next meal. A gull swooped for the crusts, catching them on the wing. Six-ten. A cluster of black dots showed on the horizon. He put the glasses on them and determined their course. It was approximately the same as his own, southwest by

167

west. He opened the throttle again, keeping the fishing boats in focus. The motor thundered under the hatch, driving the small craft at full speed. He was near enough to the boats to make out the Montorese markings on the sails. The small fleet was strung out half a mile away. There were no more than a dozen boats, lying low in the water. He could see the men sorting and gutting on deck. The gull sensed offal and looped away with a powerful beating of wings. He had a momentary sense of loss. The bird had kept him company through the night.

He spun the wheel slightly, steering a diagonal course toward the fleet. Coral outcrops marked a line of surf near the shore. A strip of yellow sand separated ocean from dense jungle vegetation. He was no longer worried about patrol boats. What he had to watch for was the Guardia Nacional. Behind the swampland and coffee hills, the peaks of the Sierra Araña divided the country east and west. The mosquito coast was uninhabited on the north side of the estuary. Guardia patrols would be thin in the area. He was a hundred yards from the fishing boats now. He cut his speed, just holding way. The bulging nets on the decks flashed silver in the early sunlight. He called a greeting. A man waved but beyond that no one took any notice. The men were preoccupied with their catch. *Rosa Negra* wallowed in their wake.

The driving spray tightened the skin of his body. His night had been sleepless but he was completely untired. A mixture of fear, hate and excitement sustained him. Drury had said it — he couldn't *afford* to fail. The enormity of his task no longer disturbed him. Montoro showed as a cluster of sugarloaves perched on five hills. The first ferry was crossing the bay from his home village. As often as he thought about it, the upheaval in his life perplexed him. It could so easily have been avoided. That first lie about the films had started everything. Now the gap was too wide — it was too late for either the truth or explanation. He was up against a ring of faceless men whose only justification was expediency. Expediency had broken up his home, made a prisoner of his wife, brought death to two men. There was no one he could turn to — not even Gregorio. The kind of loyalty he demanded was too much to expect from a friend.

Rosa Negra was dropping back imperceptibly. The mouth of the estuary was hard on his starboard. Muddy water flowed upstream, the brackish mixture ebbing back into the creeks dotting the southern shore of the river. The bluffs there boasted plantations of dogwood and savannah pines. Dotted among them were gracious houses built in colonial days, impervious to change or time. One of these belonged to Donna Rafaela Paláu. He pointed the bow into the silt-laden water. Alligators lay supine on the sandbanks. The ugly snouts of others broke the surface. He kept the cruiser in the deepest channels. Half-throttle gave him enough way against the sluggish current. There were no other boats, nothing in sight that was human. The rapids were a couple of miles upstream.

The northern shore was a dark-green wilderness strident with the noise of parrots, inhabited by snakes, lizards and caimans. He steered toward the island. Clumps of palms grew down to the water. He came in as close as he could without beaching the boat. The fringe of sand was littered with bleached bones, relics of swollen carcasses dragged out of the river by the alligators. He rounded a promontory and ran the cruiser up a creek overgrown with oleander bushes. He cut the motor. The scene was unbelievably peaceful. A clearing was ringed with eucalyptus trees. Their quick growth had outstripped that of the palms. There were no flies here, no mosquitoes. The island was perfectly silent save for the rattling of the eucalyptus leaves. He tied along the wooden landing stage. Lizards scuttled away as he stepped ashore. A small stone cabin stood in the center of the clearing. Bougainvillea grew like a weed. It hung on the porch and windows in purple and mauve ropes.

He walked over to the cabin. The windows were shuttered. A spider the size of a dollar piece eyed him from a web spun across the doorway. He flicked it off with the end of a stick. Its bite was a guaranteed fortnight of raging fever with the danger of partial paralysis. The door key was hanging on a nail. Paláu's father had built the cabin as a refuge. Part of the country's constitution had been written there. His son had never been interested in the place. There had been a few parties there but the lawyer rarely visited the island.

Macneil turned the key. There was one big room and an annex with a kitchen. He partially unfastened a shutter. A law-office desk and chair faced the jungle side of the river. There was a studio couch, no phone, no light other than that from kerosene lamps. Drinking water was brought from the mainland. He peeped into the kitchen.

Ants had invaded the zinc-lined food store. Inside a closet were shoes spotted with mildew. The smell of the river permeated the cabin. A rusty machete stood in the sink, symbol of sporadic attacks on the encroaching undergrowth. No servant was allowed on the island. It was probably months since anyone had landed there.

The location was ideal. The cabin was concealed from both shores yet accessible. He took the machete outside. The spare dinghy had been dragged onto the bank and was lying upside down. The oars were underneath. He crossed the clearing and started hacking off lengths of young green eucalyptus. He spread these over the deck and wheelhouse. The boat was completely concealed now — even from the air. He checked the fuel gauges. The reserve tank was untouched. He tried the starter, switching off immediately. *Rosa Negra* was ready for her return run. He yawned and stretched, tired suddenly. He had a few things going for him still. The element of surprise and all that jazz. Twenty past seven. He went back into the house. His clothes were stiff with salt. He took them off and stretched out on the couch. His eyes closed almost at once. A door opened at the end of a tunnel echoing with doubts.

He waked from a deep sleep, struggling up and straining his ears. All he heard was the scream of the parrots across the river. It was past noon. He had slept for nearly four hours. He locked up the house and put the key back in its hiding place. He sculled the dinghy out into the open water and rounded the tip of the island. Alligators had ousted the turtles from the sandbanks. They basked in the fierce heat, their putrid smell poisoning the air. Shoals of tiny colored fish cruised beyond the striking oars. Sweat plastered his shirt to his back. The snarled savannah roots along the southern shore were exposed and bleached the tone of ivory. He poled the dinghy in between them and tied up. He climbed out onto damp sand. Mosquitoes lifted in clouds, striking at his neck and hands as he climbed to higher ground. A stone wall rose in front of him. Beyond it lay the ordered peace of Donna Rafaela's gardens. He followed the line of the wall, fending off the stabbing insects. He headed for the telephone poles that marked the curve of the marginal highway. The gun weighed heavy in his pants pocket. He had long since accepted the inevitability of ultimate violence. He clambered up the bank to the cactus-lined highway. The bridge he had crossed with the Jew flashed silver a quarter-mile away. He flopped in the shade, out of sight of the occasional passing car. It was a couple of hours before a bus appeared. It slowed for his summons and he climbed aboard. There was no room to sit. The bus came from the hills and the occupants smelled like it. The blinds were drawn against the glare of the sun. This choked the windows. The stench was outrageous. He stood eight uncomfortable miles, wedged between two country priests. He dropped off the bus near the bullring. It was five past two and Saturday. All the stores were closed. A few seamen were at the taco stands. Otherwise the embarcadero was deserted. He strolled across and bought himself a cone of maize flour filled with peppered ground meat. He took it to the shade of a hoarding and ate there, staring out over the bay at the village that had been his home. Stage one of his plan was complete. He was alive and well in Ciudad de Montoro. But if he didn't get off the streets, he wouldn't last another hour. Not only P.I.D.E. would be looking for him. Every guy in town with a pistol and a whistle would be out bounty-hunting. He brushed the crumbs from his clothes and stood up. The sun was directly overhead. The white buildings reflected its heat. The vertical rays glittered on the sparkling waters. He put on the straw hat and dark glasses and walked across the concourse. The bar was cool inside — filled with the tang of grilled prawns, the yeasty smell of beer. The patrons were waterfront characters and incurious. The floor at their feet was littered with the debris of shellfish. Macneil took his beer to the far end of the counter. There was a phone there and a directory. He opened it, looking for the entry he needed. The name Zuimárraga appeared seven times but not with the right initial. The general's number was unlisted. Weber's was prominent. Zuimárraga would have to be located in some other way. *Gregorio*, he thought suddenly — the lawyer would certainly know. Getting hold of Paláu wouldn't be difficult. The next entry he found was in heavy black type.

POLICÍA IN DEFENSA DEL ESTADO
QUARTEL-GENERAL PALACIO DE SAN VINCENTE

He dialed, looking along the bar. The men there were still talking at one another loudly. He lowered his own voice. The answer was more or less as he expected. No information could be given on the telephone. He sensed

173

that the seconds were being stretched deliberately, that the man was holding the line for the call to be traced. He replaced the handset, threw a coin on the counter and left the bar hurriedly. The glare outside was relentless. It was the hour of the siesta. A giant hand seemed to have combed the streets, leaving them empty. Fountains played between the newly erected stands on the Avenida de Libertad. An occasional workman lay there on his back, snoring. The note was expectancy rather than somnolence. As if people were waiting in walled patios for the signal to surge out onto the sidewalks.

Traffic signals blinked on and off, controlling the sparse traffic. He held up a hand, catching a cruising cab. The driver took him to the quiet square facing the cathedral. The great doors stood open. Peasants with brown stone faces were propped against the wall, a day's bus ride from home. Others were asleep on the steps, their heads on baskets of palm crosses. The amplified voice of a priest rose in exhortation inside. Macneil ducked into a narrow street devoted to the sale of church furnishings. The windows were filled with plaster saints and gilded madonnas. There were hand-woven altar cloths from the mountain villages, freshly varnished *prie-dieus*. All the stores were closed except the last. A bell tinkled as he pushed the door open. The air inside smelled of camphor. The shelves were stacked with shovel hats and cassocks. A tailor's model displayed the latest in priests' regalia. A man climbed out of a chair where he had been nodding. His voice and manner were those of a deacon.

"I want a *penitente*'s robe," Macneil said awkwardly. It

was a strange feeling, standing in the shadow of the cathedral, a gun stuffed in his waistband. "For tonight," he added.

The owner of the shop walked around Macneil, finger and thumb holding his lower lip. He opened a large chest.

"Which guild?"

Macneil felt his face reddening. "I'm not sure. It's for a friend."

The man clucked musty disapproval. "But the color, señor. You must have the right color! This is a serious matter."

"I'm pretty certain that it's black," Macneil answered. "In fact I'm sure of it. He's about my size."

The shopkeeper dragged a robe from the chest. He held it up against the Canadian. The long full sleeves dropped to the wrists. The hem of the robe fell to Macneil's ankles. The girdle was made of half-inch rope. The eye-slitted hood covered the head completely. It was impossible to wear the robe without the hood. Macneil left the store carrying the paper-wrapped package under his arm. A network of narrow streets led to the Plaza Mayor. It was a few minutes past three. He was betting on Paláu's inexorable timetable. Six days a week found him at the Bello Mundo barbershop, the first customer of the afternoon. The lawyer's blue Packard was parked under the trees. Macneil stepped into a phone booth. Curtained windows hid the interior of the Bello Mundo, but Macneil knew it well. His mind placed Paláu in the third chair from the door, lolling like a pasha, a manicurist holding his hand, his head wrapped in steamed towels.

Macneil dialed the barbershop. He gave the reception-ist the lawyer's name. He heard a click as the phone was plugged in by the lawyer's chair — then his friend's voice.

"Paláu — *dígame!*"

Macneil looked across the square. He spoke in English. "I'm in the booth opposite. Listen to me carefully. You know where Zuimárraga lives — or you can find out. I want the address."

The rhythm of the lawyer's voice was unruffled. He might have been responding to an inquiry about the weather.

"There's a P.I.D.E. car sitting outside. A black Volks-wagen with two men in it. Are you completely out of your mind?"

"Yes!" Macneil's voice tightened. "I can see your friends from here. Don't worry about it. Do I get that address or not?"

He heard the whine of hair clippers. A girl laughed. The lawyer rasped his throat clear.

"Get off the streets, Dougal. Stay there till it's dark and then go home. They've taken the watch off your house. Wait there till I get word to you. It's your only chance — don't spoil it. Think of Pilar. I'm going to the presi-dent himself."

"You'll be wasting your time," Macneil said grimly. "Where does Zuimárraga live?"

A sound of despair terminated the lawyer's sudden si-lence. "I'll spell it out," he said slowly. *"Avenida de la Fuente, four-two*. It'll be right at the top of the hill and there's bound to be a guard. You must be crazy. I'm going

straight home from here. I'll be there if you can get word
to me."

Macneil replaced the receiver. Enormous old lime trees
dappled the square with shade. Children were racing past
the benches where old men still dozed. One of the
P.I.D.E. agents detached himself from the Volkswagen
and stationed himself in a nearby doorway. A woman
tapped on the door of the phone booth. Macneil pushed
out, walking as casually as he could. His line brought him
within ten feet of the parked Volkswagen. The man at the
wheel was sucking his back teeth. His partner in the doorway affected to be reading a newspaper. Macneil strolled
on, resisting the urge to turn around. His palms were
sweating and his stomach shaking but the piece of fool-
hardiness had restored his confidence. He turned onto a
short street that intersected the Avenida de Libertad. The
foyer of the Vox Cinema was crowded with matinee patrons. The usual pair of cops loitered in the entrance,
enigmatic behind outsize dark glasses. He bought a balcony ticket and sat through the newsreel and feature. It
was two and a half hours later when the cinema emptied.
He made his way to the bar, smoked a couple of cigarettes
over a beer and waited for the second show to start. This
time he sat downstairs. The interval over, he slipped
through the darkened theater to the lavatory. He locked
himself inside and changed into the black robe. Nothing
was left to view but his shoes and hands. He felt his way
out to the passage. The sound track echoed emptily. He
lifted the bar on the door at the end and stepped onto the
car park. It was hot under the hood. It was difficult to

keep the slits positioned in front of his eyes. He resettled the robe and tied the rope girdle tighter. It was almost nine and still light. The streets were bedlam. Entry had been barred to the Avenida de Libertad. Drivers were leaving their cars where they stopped — in the middle of the road or on the sidewalks. Their one thought seemed to be to reach the stands a block away.

The processions were already winding up the broad avenue toward the palace. Small girls dressed in white and carrying bouquets, pokerfaced Indians, a guild of boys dressed in sailors' uniforms. The sidewalks were crowded with the religious. Franciscan friars with fat faces — a party of nuns, fluttering like gray moths. The hooded robes were everywhere. A group a hundred or so strong was straggling along at the tail of the procession. A priest with the eyes of a fanatic whipped them with a hoarse voice from the sidelines. Most of them were without shoes. Some carried chains, one a wooden cross. They shuffled on to the sound of the drumbeat. An escort of gum-chewing motorcycle cops, helmeted and goggled, fetched up the rear. Macneil pushed his way through the crowd till he reached the edge of the stand. As the group of *penitentes* neared, he stepped over the rope cordon and joined them.

GENERAL
ILIDIO ZUIMÁRRAGA

THE DRIVE HOME took more than an hour, four times as long as usual. The Avenida de Libertad was closed to cars. The downtown intersections looked like parking lots. Haphazard dumping of vehicles made passage through them impossible. The ministry Mercedes nudged its way slowly across the city. An occasional policeman on traffic duty recognized it and came to life. Whistles shrilled, holding the signals. But for the most part it was a succession of stops and starts, of interminable waits as one procession after another wound down the hills toward the waterfront. The main assembly place was the concourse in front of the bullring. From there the parades would march to the presidential palace.

It was well past seven when he reached the beginning of the slope that led to his home. San Fermin was a small wooded hill, three kilometers west of the city limits. The five hundred hectares had been carefully landscaped. A ribbon of hardtop snaked up through gardens sweet with the smell of *huelo-de-noche* trees. There were no sidewalks, no houses visible from the road till the crest of the hill was reached. A turning circle there offered a panoramic view of the city. Scrubland surrounded the base of

179

the hill, segregating its affluence from the shacks built at
the back of the bus sheds. The people living on San
Fermin were located in pecking order. A banker lived in
the bottom villa. A hundred yards above him was a coffee
planter from the highlands. Above this, the ornate house
of the minister of tourism. On the crest of the hill were
two villas, Zuimárraga's and the one belonging to Don
Pasquale Cortes. Each owed its position to chance rather
than merit. Don Pasquale's wife was the president's sister.
The general's father-in-law had owned and developed the
estate. The house had come as a wedding present. He
turned the car in a tight circle and left it in front of the
ornate iron gates. The grass behind the hedges was wet,
the air cool and watered. Two gardeners were winding up
the hoses, bare-legged, their heads covered with straw
hats the size of small cartwheels. He picked a mauve orchid from a bed near the wall. He held the waxlike petals
close to his nose, sniffing its cloying scent. It was a time of
day that he enjoyed usually. By nature he was lazy. Years
of experience had given him the ability to suspend all
thought of work at a given moment. It was Weber who
was the departmental conscience.

Memory of Weber had become deeply disturbing. The
fact that he could find no real ground for this only added
to Zuimárraga's concern. The German's methods were
certainly ruthless. So were those of the rabble-rousers
from Cuba. Zuimárraga cleared his mind of the problem.
Perhaps the real reason for his malaise was that he dis-
liked Weber — nothing more, nothing less. He looked up,
hearing his name spoken. A bear of a man was walking

along the veranda. He was wearing a short-sleeved shirt outside his trousers. The outline of the gun beneath it showed as he came down the steps.

Zuimárraga acknowledged his salute mechanically. He had had the same men as bodyguards for the last four years. His flock, he called them, aware of their problems and ambitions. He saw himself as the protector rather than the protected.

"Donna Carmen?" he inquired.

The bodyguard's dark face flashed a smile. "In the patio, Señor General, with the children."

Zuimárraga pointed at the car. "We're going into the city. You might as well come too. There'll be nobody here but the maid."

He pushed the patio gate open. The two small girls flew at him, clutching his legs and clamoring for attention. He lifted them up in turn, holding each above his head till she screamed with delight. They looked at him with Carmen's eyes, scrubbed and sweet in their short flowered dresses. He pushed them into the house, lumbering after them with mock ferocity.

"For them kisses, for me nothing." His wife's placid smile reproached him gently.

He touched his lips to her cheek and stuck the orchid in her smooth dark hair. He dropped into the chair under the pepper tree, kicking off his shoes.

"I've got to go back to the ministry for a couple of hours. I'll take you and the children in with me. We have the same seats as usual. Row D in the Presidential Stand. I'll meet you there afterward."

She took the engraved admission card and fanned herself with it. "Father Loyola telephoned again. He's expecting you at eleven o'clock. How long do you think you'll be at confession?"

He curled his toes, looking down at his belly. He tightened the muscles tentatively. Nothing happened. Two inches of flesh still bulged above his belt.

"Not long," he said, frowning. "I live in a state of grace."

His wife took the news with reservations. "That is very near blasphemy. By the way, how's the girl who is having the baby?"

"All right," he said carelessly. He picked his shoes up and rose. "We'd better get dressed."

His wife swept an armful of toys into her lap. "I've told Paquita that she can come to the carnival tomorrow. You tell her too or she won't enjoy a minute of it. You terrify her."

He grunted and padded over to the kitchen door. The girl was bending over a basket of ironing. He could see her unbound breasts, brown and firm under her gingham uniform. She straightened up self-consciously. He put some coins on the table.

"For tomorrow. Buy yourself a pair of stockings." There was a pencil and pad on the dresser. He wrote on it and gave her the slip. "Read it!"

She held the paper nervously, composing the words soundlessly till her voice found confidence.

"In case of a telephone call, the general will be at the ministry until ten o'clock. After that he is attending confession at the cathedral. A message can be left at the presbytery, in care of Father Loyola, if the matter is important."

She smoothed the piece of paper into a small square and looked at him apprehensively. He took her ear between thumb and forefinger and tweaked it. He shaved again and was half an hour in the bathroom. He dressed in a black silk suit, cummerbund and white shirt. The reflection in the mirror satisfied him. A man, he thought, of mature dignity. He went into the adjoining room. His wife was coiling the last rope of hair on top of her head.

"Why did you ask me about that girl?" he asked bluntly.

She skewered her hair with a tortoiseshell comb, speaking over her shoulder.

"Because I knew you were interested in her."

He stood in the doorway, breathing heavily as she searched for missals and a black lace mantilla. He rose to the bait as he always did.

"I don't know that I understand you. I've never even met the woman."

She turned around slowly on the stool, settling a shoulder strap. Her eyes were wide.

"*Aleee*, Ilidio, you are such a liar!"

His cheeks flapped with indignation. He pulled the door shut. "I shall be grateful for a direct answer, Carmen. Do you think that I deceive you?"

"I am certain of it," she said coolly. "Do you suppose me to be a complete fool? Do you want names?"

"*Names?*" he repeated dangerously.

She nodded. "Let's take this year. Señorita Calderon,

183

the daughter of that old, old friend of yours from Costa Rica. Then the girl from the ministry, how was she called? The one who spent her free time falling off horses. I'm sure there are others."

His voice rose to a bellow. "Lies, woman, lies! The mother of my children harboring such thoughts — it's indecent. Have you no respect?"

Suddenly he saw himself again in the mirror. This time, old and fat, the veins bulging in his forehead.

"You'll do yourself an injury," his wife said calmly. She gave him one of the prayer books. "Examine your conscience before you go to see Father Loyola. I've marked the appropriate passages."

He stuffed the missal into his pocket and wrenched the door open. His daughters answered his call, running across the hall into his arms. He wrapped them to him, holding them closely, glaring defiance at Carmen. She ignored it completely, retying the bow in the younger girl's hair. She smiled at her husband sweetly.

"Shall we go?"

He slammed the front door hard behind them. She moved out to the car majestically, the children before her. They sat in the back, the bodyguard in front next to Zuimárraga. The big black sedan glided down the hill. Zuimárraga cocked an eye at the driving mirror. His wife was still smiling. He drove to the Parque Central. The crowds assembling before the bullring had broken, part of them spilling into the park. A group of *penitentes* was standing in close formation. A priest was addressing them from the bandstand. Zuimárraga's cheeks sagged with disapproval.

He had no time for this hysterical exhibitionism. A few more hours would see them off the leash, the priest included. There was higher incidence of murder, rape and theft on the first day of carnival than at any other time in the year. He turned around sharply, recognizing the car that had pulled in behind them.

"There's your sister," he said shortly.

His wife opened the door on her side. The two girls came around to Zuimárraga's window. Each kissed him and curtseyed. He gave them both the same injunction to obedience and good behavior. His wife gathered her two daughters. She looked at him placidly, cool and motherly. He remembered a girl of quicksilver, offering surrender with passion. He still loved her. One no longer spoke of such matters.

"We'll wait in the stand for you. Give my best wishes to Father Loyola."

She smiled and he lifted his hand. His dignity was completely restored. He resolved that in the future his adventures would be conducted with more care. He drove back across town to the ministry. A skeleton staff slept there, his aide among them. He let himself in through the side door. His secretary had left a bound folder on the desk. The general lowered himself into a chair and read the label on the cover.

A REPORT BY THE DELEGATE OF THE REPUBLIC OF
MONTORO TO A CONFERENCE OF SECURITY CHIEFS
PANAMA   APRIL 1969

185

Print added importance to his words. He scanned the report and the letter attached.

EXCELLENCY!
I have the honor to submit the following report for approval and subscribe myself Your Excellency's loyal servant,
Minister of the Interior
ILIDIO ZUIMÁRRAGA

He signed the letter and threw the report in a basket. It had to be delivered at the palace on Monday. He was still at work when his aide rapped and entered.

"I saw the light, General. I'm glad that I caught you. It's Señor Paláu again. He's telephoned four times since you left."

Zuimárraga looked at the clock. It was a quarter-past ten. Darkness spread beyond the windows. The city reverberated with the sound of church bells. The general shrugged.

"I told you what to do about that."

"I know, sir." His aide's voice was apologetic. "But he's talking about going to the president."

Zuimárraga stood on his toes, stretching. The maid's hand had been heavy with chilies tonight. A bonfire was burning under his navel. He swallowed a bismuth tablet.

"These lawyers are worse than the military, Carlos. If he calls again, I suppose you'd better make an appointment for Monday. I'll have to think of something to shrink his head a little."

He switched off the lights and let himself out as he had come. Forty-eight hours he had given Weber. Half of these were already gone. The thought was doubly disturbing. He lifted his eyes to the galaxy of stars overhead. And now to confession. The idea gave him a strange prescience — a lover going to a tryst. His mouth buckled wryly at the image. Father Loyola would hardly appreciate it. He climbed into the car and started the motor.

DOUGAL MACNEIL

THE HILL ROSE before him, pastoral in the moonlight. He pushed the stolen bicycle into the shelter of some trees and laid it on its side. No one but a couple of stray dogs had noticed the hooded cyclist pedaling across the wasteland. The animals had followed him to the bottom of the hill, yelping their heads off. He bent down as if reaching for a stone. They backed off, turned tail and ran. The quiet avenue wound up between low walls and hedges. There were no streetlamps. The gardens were landscaped into the contours of the slopes, the houses hidden from the road. The grade grew steeper. The screams of cats fighting carried on the wind. It was mercifully cooler inside the hood. He had achieved the knack of positioning his eyes behind the slits. He stopped a few yards from the crest of the hill. Two houses faced one another across a turning circle. Zuimárraga's was the one on the right.

He vaulted over an iron chain onto grass. He worked his way along, his eyes on the villa opposite. It was a large one-story building with an arched veranda and a red roof. A light was showing somewhere at the back. The moon illuminated the garden and hedge at the front. The garage doors were up, the space inside empty. He stood quite still, watching, for fully five minutes. The empty garage proved nothing. A man like Zuimárraga could still be at home. All he had to do was take the phone off the hook and a dozen cars would be there. The front door seemed to be opening slowly. He lifted the gun in readiness but the movement was in his mind. The breeze rattled through the trees behind him. There was no sign of the guard Paláu had warned him about. He groped for a rock and lobbed it like a hand grenade. He heard it clatter down the roof and fall to the ground. Nobody challenged. There was no suspicious movement. He jumped the chain barrier and ran for the garage. There was a door set in the back wall. He turned the handle slowly, taking the weight as the door inched open. He was standing in a high-walled patio. A pepper tree grew in the center. An awning gently creaked beneath it. A blond doll propped in a chair stared at him with sightless eyes. Somehow he hadn't expected children. There were windows on his right. The light he had seen came from the last one.

He crept forward, ducking as low as he could as he reached the drawn curtains. He straightened up, peeping through the crack into a large kitchen. A brown-skinned girl in a white shift was washing plates in the sink. Her eyes were vague. Her hair bristled with metal curlers. One long step took him to the door. He rapped on it imperatively. He could hear her catch her breath. He rapped again, kicking against the wood.

Her voice was shrill. "Who is it?"

"Open up," he said. "There's a message for the general."

She was angling her head behind the curtain, trying to get a better look at him. He moved farther out of sight. The bolts were withdrawn. As the door opened, he went in hard behind his shoulder. He grabbed at the girl quickly. It was like wrestling with a bale of barbed wire. Her fingers seemed to be tipped with fishhooks. They raked at his hooded head uselessly. He forced her away from the bread knife, shoved her down on a chair and kicked the patio door shut. He put the barrel of the gun against her head. She took a deep breath, screwing up her eyes and shaping a scream. Her mouth closed as he held a warning finger in front of it.

"What's your name?"

Her eyes flicked sideways. "Paquita."

She was sitting with her knees locked together, her arms crossed over her breasts. The acrid smell of fear exuded from her body. He put the gun away. It had served its purpose. He guessed they were alone in the house. He lifted her chin with his hand.

"Listen to me, Paquita. Answer the questions and nothing will happen to you. I want to know how many people are living in the house, where they are and when you expect them back. The truth, now."

She wrapped herself still tighter in a defensive huddle. "Jesús María," she said forlornly.

He shook her head gently. "How many people?"

"Five," she said in a small voice. "The general, Donna Carmen, the children and me. They've all gone into town."

He took his fingers away from her face. "What about the bodyguard?"

"He went with them."

He bent down again, bringing his hooded head close to hers. "If you're lying, I'll kill you."

"It's true," she said despairingly. "They've gone to the processions. If anyone phoned I was to give a message. It's on the desk in the sitting room."

He pushed her in front of him into a big room with lemon-colored curtains and cushions. There were two telephones on the desk. He read the note on the pad and put it in his pocket. The Fate Sisters were at his side, whispering. He knew exactly what he had to do.

"Where's your room, chica?" he asked.

Her small square face was ugly with tears. She looked around wildly, as if rape was abroad. Time was running out. He grabbed her from behind and lifted her off her feet. He carried her, struggling, into the first room across the hallway. He threw her down on the bed. He was breathing heavily. He was in no shape for this sort of thing. It was as well she was past making resistance. She lay on the bed, twitching, tears oozing from her tightly shut eyes.

He ripped a sheet lengthways and tied her wrists behind her back — then her ankles. He leaned over her, his tone threatening.

"I'll be watching from outside. Move as much as a finger and I'll be back to cut your throat."

He tiptoed away into the living room. He yanked the two phones out of the wall, leaving the broken wires dangling from the desk. He let himself out onto the veranda. It was absolutely quiet except for a cicada rasping away in the bushes. No lights showed anywhere. All the villas looked temporarily deserted. The wooded hill was remote from the city. He dragged off the robe and rolled it in a bundle. The air was mercifully cool on his face. He dragged it into his lungs in great gulps. He'd cycle across town as he was. The cops had other things to do at this hour than look for him. He trotted down the hill, his rubber soles making no sound on the hardtop. He dragged the bicycle out of the weeds. The carrier had a spring-loaded clip. He bundled the robe into a paper sack and fastened it behind the saddle. He wobbled out onto the road. Balance was better when he pedaled harder. He rode through quiet suburban streets devoid of pedestrians. It was Saturday night but all public transport had stopped running at eight o'clock. There was very little traffic circulating. He passed a water-cannon truck drawn up behind a screen of trees. The show of force was no more than a reminder. Any trouble would come later, at the height of carnival. The sidewalks were blocked with cars. Another ten minutes brought him into the streets behind the palace. The police were more numerous here but still passive. They stood in cautious knots, allowing the crowds to surge toward the Avenida de Libertad unchecked. He crossed it a few blocks north of the point where he had stolen the bicycle. The people around him were shouting and sweating. Children were held high in the air to see the passing processions. Someone let off a premature firecracker. A police horse reared to the screaming of women. But the crowd was still good-humored.

He pumped on up the hill. Block after block was deserted. The storefronts blazed on empty sidewalks. Not a breath of air blew here. Sound hung in the ovenlike atmosphere. A blaze over the rooftops indicated the cathedral. The walls of the great building were lavender-gray in the floodlighting. The square at the side was comparatively dark. He wheeled the bicycle into an alley. He unclipped the bundled robe and left the machine where it was. He climbed the cathedral steps with aching legs. Worshipers were streaming into the great church. The atmosphere inside was thick with incense. He saw the scene with the eyes of a photographer. Votive candles flared on all sides. Peasants, off-duty police, whores and shopkeepers — all kneeled together, their lips working in silent prayer. He pushed through those who were standing till he was behind the giant organ. There was less pressure there. The cathedral was already half-full though midnight mass was an hour and a half away. Hooded figures were everywhere. He could see the row of confessional boxes over on the right of the nave. He started edging his way toward them. The side altars were rich with gilt and color. More candles blazed in front of each. The confessionals were hung with black curtains. There were eight of them. Cards pushed into small metal frames identified the priests who were hearing confession. The last frame held the card he was looking for.

FATHER LOYOLA S.J.
ESPAÑOL Y PORTUGUEZ

He put his ear against the curtain. There was no sound inside. Voices told him that some of the other boxes at least were occupied. The cathedral clock boomed another quarter hour. The noise shivered in the high vaulted ceiling. Half-past ten. He slipped around the boxes and left the church through a side door. The fountain across the square ran like mercury. The presbytery was behind the line of parked cars. A dark stone building in darkness except for two lighted windows, one up, one down. Macneil moved closer. The man in the downstairs room was sitting with his back to the window. The top of his head just showed above the chair. A circle was shaven in the crown of springy white hair. The room was like a study. There were books and a portrait of Pope John. More than that he couldn't see. He padded up the steps. The door handle turned easily. A crack of light extended over the dim hall, coming from the room where the priest was sitting. Macneil made no noise on the polished boards. He pushed the door back very gently with the heel of his hand.

The priest spoke without turning his head. "Come in."

Macneil showed himself. "You wouldn't be Father Loyola? The front door was open and it's an emergency."

The priest swung around slowly. He was a frail man with prominent eyes bulging under heavy lids. He must have been over seventy, wearing a plain dark suit and a clerical collar. The breviary he had been reading fell into his lap.

"I am Father Loyola, yes. What is it, my son?"

Someone was walking around upstairs. The priest was looking curiously at the paper sack under Macneil's arm. The Canadian glanced down. The bundled-up robe was showing. He pushed it back out of sight.

"There's been an accident, Father. It's Señora Zuimárraga. They want you to go to the house immediately. The doctor's on his way."

The risk was a calculated one. It would take the Jesuit an hour to discover the truth and act on it. And the phones up on the hill were out of action.

Father Loyola's fingers were playing with his rosary. He weighed the beads in the palm of his hand, his face thoughtful.

"Why are you lying to me, my son? What have you come here for?"

"I don't understand, Father. There's been an accident. Señora Zuimárraga is asking for you."

The old priest shook his head. "I spoke to her on the telephone no more than ten minutes ago."

Macneil moved swiftly, drawing the curtains and shutting the door to the hall. He turned to face the priest, aiming the barrel of the gun at the other man's stomach.

"I didn't want it this way, Father. I have no choice. On your feet now and keep away from that bell push."

They heard the steps coming down the stairs at the same time. Macneil moved to the priest's side. He shifted his aim at the door. A woman called from the hall.

"It's getting on for eleven, Father. You told me to remind you. I'm going out now otherwise I won't get a seat."

Macneil was staring over the priest's head. Father Loyola's hands were held above his head but his voice was steady.

"*Bueno*, Maria! Make sure you have your key with you."

The front door was slammed. Macneil stepped to the

curtain. He watched the housekeeper hurry away, adjusting a mantilla over her gray head. The priest's arms were trembling violently. He excused himself with a nervous smile.

"They grow tired quickly."

"Put them down," Macneil said impatiently. The priest's gentle reason irked him. He'd been forced into attacking an old and defenseless man. That was reality, whatever the reasons to justify it. He drifted over to the desk. There was only one entry in the day-journal.

Confession 11 p.m. Gen-Z.

Father Loyola's expression was as shaky as his arms. "There is nothing here to steal, my son. What money I have is in the desk. Take it and go. I shall pray for you."

Macneil turned the handle and stepped into the hall. "I don't need your prayers, Father."

The old priest extended his empty hands persuasively. "Give me the weapon, my son. You need more than prayers. I can tell. We can talk of this."

Macneil backed off, feeling behind him for the catch on the door. A lavatory was annexed to the cloakroom. The one window was solidly barred. He jerked his head inside. The priest obeyed. The look that passed between them told the Canadian that the old man had guessed somewhere near the truth. He turned the key in the lock and wiped his forehead. The face in the mirror was that of a stranger. The misery and fear of the last few days was beginning to show. The eyes and mouth were strained.

He donned the robe again and left the presbytery. He reached the confessional boxes, going back through the side entrance. It was five minutes to eleven. Worshipers were kneeling in the pews, waiting their turn for confession. The backs of the boxes were in deep shadow. No one noticed Macneil slip into the last one. It was pitch-dark inside. He put his eye to the fretted wood screen. A chink in the curtain on the other side allowed a view of the nearest pew. A stout man was kneeling in the end seat. Macneil recognized him from the pictures. It was Zuimárraga all right. He lumbered up on his feet as the clock bell tolled eleven. He genuflected in the aisle and came toward Macneil with his hands clasped and head bent. The curtain dragged along the rail. A dull thud sounded as the general's knees hit the floor. Macneil brought his mouth close to the screen.

"There's a gun pointing at your head. Think of your wife and children and take it nice and easy."

The words were melodramatic. Situations seemed to provide their own dialogue. He could see nothing in the darkness. He sensed rather than saw the movement. Zuimárraga was getting to his feet.

"Walk around the box and wait in the aisle." Macneil's voice was a hoarse whisper. "You're a dead man if you try to be a hero."

A low mumble came from the adjoining boxes. Macneil slipped outside. Boys in surplices were lighting candles on the High Altar. The vast cathedral rustled with muted sound. The aisle he was standing in was in semi-darkness. This was the moment. If Zuimárraga was going to make a break, he'd do it now. A single shout would be enough. The whole place would be in turmoil. Leather scraped

197

over stone. The general appeared from the far side of the boxes, walking like a man testing ice. Each step was slow and tentative. Macneil could hear the other man's labored breathing. He stepped away from the wall. The flapping sleeve of the robe concealed the gun in his hand. The general came to a halt. There was enough light to see his half-open mouth — the look of shocked disbelief as he glanced down at the gun pressed against his ribs.

The thudding in Macneil's ears was the beating of his own heart. Her jerked his hooded head at the alcove behind them.

"Through this door."

He ripped off the robe as they stepped into the alcove. He threw it in a corner. Suddenly the organ pealed. He opened and shut the door on the swelling sound of the music. The barest whisper of wind stirred the torrid air. The study light was still burning in the presbytery. The fountain flashed in indigo shadow. The small square lay quiet. Zuimárraga was standing with his arms hanging helplessly. His whole weight appeared to be concentrated in the upper half of his body. His eyes were the only things alive in his flabby face. The apprehension in them was echoed in his voice.

"I know who you are — you won't get away with it."

Again the melodrama — the phrase a cliché from a thousand forgotten movies. Only this time it wasn't true. The Canadian's mouth was confident.

"I'll get away with it. I've got you as a guardian angel. Where's your car?"

Zuimárraga indicated the black sedan parked on the far

side of the square. His features were molded in an expression of resignation. Macneil saw the silhouette of a man's head and shoulders in the front seat of the car.

"Who's that?" he asked sharply. He was starting to get edgy again and there was nothing he could do about it.

Zuimárraga shifted a shoulder. "My bodyguard. He'll do what I tell him."

Macneil's face was grim. "Let's hope so for your sake. You and I are going to walk over there, acting naturally. This gun will be in your back. I'll kill you if I have to. I think you know why."

They walked down the steps and approached the car from the rear. Macneil's gun hand was concealed by the general's body. Zuimárraga leaned through the open window. His escort nodded briefly, climbed out and saluted. His eyes rested on Macneil incuriously. They listened to his footsteps die in the distance. Macneil ran his fingers over Zuimárraga's clothing, feeling for a weapon.

"Get behind the wheel," he ordered. There was no gun in the glove compartment. Nothing in the armrest but a radiophone. He shifted to face the driver. "Now listen and make no mistakes — I've come back for my wife. If I have to tear this whole town apart to get her, I'll do it."

Zuimárraga looked a badly beaten man. He shook his head very slowly.

"I tell you that it won't work. You're only digging your own grave — your wife's too. There is another way out, though. Do you trust your lawyer?"

Macneil's thumb massaged the notched grip of the gun. "As long as I've got you I don't need him."

Sound of the cathedral bell rolled across the quiet square. Zuimárraga crossed himself and touched his thumb to his lips.

"I have an idea. First of all I have to know what it is you want from me, Señor Macneil."

The Canadian's smile was sardonic. The faceless men were human after all. All you needed to reach them was a gun.

"That's simple. I want my wife. We're going to see Weber together. He's at home, waiting for me. You're going to tell him that my wife's to leave San Vincente alone. No escort — nothing but my wife, alone. Walking where she pleases. Once she's in this car, you're coming with us as insurance."

The general's bewilderment showed in his face. "Coming with you where?"

"To Puerto Vedra," Macneil said quietly.

Zuimárraga leaned his head into his hands. The light from the dash shone on the balding patch in his scalp. When he finally looked up, it was with a sort of despairing dignity.

"Then you'll have to kill me. I'm telling you that your plan won't work. Weber wouldn't surrender a Castro agent if his mother's fate hung on it. There's something else. I can give orders but they wouldn't be obeyed. This is the truth, Señor Macneil. I couldn't even get in to see your wife last night."

Macneil looked at him blankly. "Did you say 'Castro agent'?"

Zuimárraga sighed. "What does it matter. You can certainly kill me but you won't achieve your object. It's a stalemate. I said there was another way out and I meant it. We'll have to work fast — take the play away from Weber. If Paláu and I can go to the president with your full confession — names, dates and places — everything you know, I think I can guarantee your freedom."

The words hit like hammer blows. "Castro-agent" — "full confession." He groped with his free hand, finding the three transparencies in his jacket pocket. He chose one at random and laid it on the seat between them.

"Take a good look at that. It's the racetrack, a couple of days ago. You'll see three men and a helicopter. One is the pilot, the second's Weber. I'm not sure about the third. Make up my mind for me."

The general picked up the print. He held it under the dashlight. He dropped the small square of cardboard as if it had scorched him.

"Martin Bormann!"

The shocked comment was out. It was too late to cover it with the subsequent flurry of words. The picture was suddenly clear in Macneil's mind. He needed no more facts. Martin Bormann, Hitler's deputy. The man said to have lived like a feudal baron, some said in Chile, others Brazil. It didn't matter. What did matter was that the war criminal wanted by Americans, Russians and Jews alike had been in Montoro and Weber was his protector.

Zuimárraga's face was red with emotion. "You've made this country your own, señor. We cannot afford a disclosure like this. Think what it would mean."

"I'm thinking," said Macneil.

201

Zuimárraga tried again. "Weber is a traitor. There's no time to lose. If you'll only trust me . . ."

Macneil cut in, his voice savage. He was up dangerously tight, beyond subterfuge or argument.

"Forget it. We're still going to Weber together. And if your methods don't work on him, you can bet mine will."

WERNER WEBER

IT WAS COOLER out on the roof. The people in the neighboring apartments were out. He sat watching the illuminated bottle on top of the next building tip and pour endlessly. The reflections reached across the roofs, bathing him in light every forty-five seconds. He moved his chair closer to the parapet and lit a cheroot. The spent match spun away through the air.

Midnight had just sounded, exploding the city into carnival. The air was full of church bells, car horns and ships' sirens. A dancing, chanting crowd moved along the street below, arms interlocked. The embarcadero was a sweep of colored lamps. Rockets fired from the marine base soared above the bay, hanging for one tantalizing second before showering the sea with brilliance.

Habit kept his back straight but Weber was tired. Body and mind needed the rest they had earned. His weary brain still continued to catalog events. His new life should have begun with Schulze's safe departure. Schulze's — no, *Bormann's!* No need to pretend any longer. The next steps had been planned with care, unknown to anyone but himself. An airplane ticket to Madrid, a meeting with the one man who would further his claims to recognition.

Then Germany once more, a place near those who were still dedicated to the old ideals. His record and ability spoke for themselves. Twenty-five years he'd waited, only to find himself close to failure. Von Ostdorf would be there first, carrying a tale of faulty security arrangements. Perhaps even worse — Bormann's obsession with treachery was bound to carry weight. Yet without the Canadian's photographs there was no proof. The whole thing could be turned to advantage even now. Von Ostdorf could still be exposed for what he was. It would be the baron who was the traitor. A man prepared to rob his country in the very hour of defeat — to jeopardize the safety of Reichsleiter Bormann from motives of jealousy. The key was Macneil and the photographs.

He tensed suddenly as a new sound invaded his consciousness. The elevator. He crossed the darkened apartment to the front door. His ear had heard right. The rattle was in the center shaft, the one that carried the penthouse express. He had removed both bulbs from the corridor but the elevator cage was lit. He watched aghast as the door opened. Zuimárraga was first to emerge, funereal in black, fear written in every line of his fat face. The Canadian followed with a gun in his hand. Three days had aged him. The toffee-streaked gray hair was wild, his mouth and eyes hard with purpose.

Weber closed the door silently. He was halfway out to the roof when he realized that the catch was still up. It was too late to go back. The two men were nearing the apartment. He made it out to the roof as the lights were snapped on inside. He could see the Canadian standing by the lamp. Zuimárraga's voice sounded relieved.

"I told you — he's not here. You've *got* to listen to me now. If you'll let me use the phone . . ."

Macneil raised his hand, pointing at the ashtray on the table. Weber's cheroot was smoldering there.

"He's here," he said grimly.

Weber edged backward through the tubbed bushes. The french windows in the next apartment were open. He stepped inside and locked them. He heard both men come out onto the roof. He watched Macneil walk to the parapet and peer down into the street. Weber tiptoed through the silent room and into the corridor. He went down the service stairs, taking them three at a time. The street beyond the forecourt was jammed with merrymakers. He ran to his car. The hood was festooned with paper streamers. He backed out, an eye cocked at the driving mirror. There was no sign of the couple in the entrance lobby.

The sheer press of bodies slowed him to walking pace. Someone was blowing a trombone in the dancing crowd. The noise was deafening. He ground on, beating off the hands that reached through the open window. The end was very near. Zuimárraga knew the truth. He wrenched the wheel, seizing his chance to go up on the sidewalk. Bollards scattered in his path. Women hurled themselves away from the car, shrieking. He drove around the fountain, through the trees and out onto the street on the other side. Some drunks were singing outside a bar. A bottle crashed against the door panel as he swung around the next intersection. He reached San Vincente in eleven minutes flat. No one was behind him. He left the car at the rear of the police buildings. To be hunted instead of the hunter was an almost forgotten experience. The big shut-tered houses stood silent in gardens made ghostly by moonlight. The downtown clamor was no more than a thin echo up here. He unlocked a small door in the back wall and crossed the cloister at the trot. Minutes counted now. Kokoscka rose from his chair unsteadily. He was unshaven and stank of liquor. Weber nodded at the floor above.

"Is she in bed?"

Kokoscka took the cigarette from his mouth. His speech was slow and blurred.

"One prisoner, all correct, Colonel."

There was a bottle under his chair. Weber took him by the lapels and shook him.

"Get a hold on yourself, man! Go up and knock at the door. Tell her to get dressed. I'll be back in a minute."

The light was burning in the woman's room when he looked back from his office. He went about his business methodically, obliterating all record of the two escaped prisoners. He unlocked the small safe behind his desk. It was empty except for a manila envelope on the bottom shelf. The documents certified his reception into the Lu-theran Church, a membership card from the Hitler *Jug-end*. The last items were his passport and a thin sheaf of United States dollars. The envelope contained the sum total of his life, times and achievements. He closed the safe again and left the key on the desk. He ran back across the lawn, looking up at the curtained window.

Kokoscka looked at him stupidly. "She's dressed,

Colonel. She says you'll have to carry her if you want to move her."

"Report to the guardhouse," Weber said quickly. "Wait there for me."

He climbed the stairs, knocked and turned the door-knob. Macneil's wife was sitting on the edge of the bed, her cap of dark hair bound with a red ribbon. Her eyes and mouth were free of makeup. The yellow dress bulged frankly. She was wearing thonged sandals and her brown legs were bare. She looked no more than seventeen. He came to a halt in front of her.

"Señora Macneil."

She met him with silent, contemptuous appraisal. He pulled the curtain aside and looked across at the guard-room. Kokoscka was weaving his way along the cloister. Weber threw her things in the bag.

"If you want to join your husband," he said shortly. "There is no time to lose."

She was around in a flash. "You're lying!"

He picked up her bag. "I'm not lying, señora. A great deal has happened since I saw you last. You might almost say that your husband and I are on the same side."

She came to her feet, fingers creeping to her throat. "I don't believe you."

"It's the truth. I'm going to take you to him. Here, give me your arm."

She moved away immediately, insisting on walking alone. They crossed the grass unseen, keeping to the shadow. She carried her swollen belly awkwardly. They skirted the wall to the small door he had used. Rusted hinges protested as he pushed it open. The street was empty, the rear lights of the Mercedes only a few feet away. He beckoned her outside and refastened the door. She swung her hair back, watching his every move. He threw her bag on the back seat and took his place beside her.

"I wasn't lying. I'm going to take you to your husband now."

She looked at him but said nothing. He tested the radiophone. The circuit was open. The big black car coasted down the hill. The sky was hung with flares. Baskets of colored lights exploded high under the stars. He drove fast, keeping clear of the center of town. The winding cutoff followed the course of a dry arroyo. Above them lay the plateau where it had all started. The racetrack buildings glimmered in the moonlight. They dropped down till the marginal highway showed ahead. He pulled the Mercedes onto the shoulder and cut the motor. Whitecaps topped the tons of crashing water. The beach shuddered under each assault. Then the ocean dragged back, leaving lacework patterns on the sand.

He picked up the phone. The communications room was skeleton-staffed after midnight. It was a couple of minutes before his call was answered. He gave the operator the number of Zuimárraga's car and waited, knuckles drumming on the rim of the steering wheel. She lit a cigarette, letting it burn away unsmoked between her fingers. The line clicked to life. Sound of a man's breathing was superimposed on the noise of a car engine.

"Zuimárraga."

Weber spoke with meaning. "He's left the country,

General. Three hours ago. Do you understand what I'm saying?"

Zuimárraga's answer was guarded. "I understand."

"Let me talk to Macneil," said Weber. He heard the phone change hands and continued. "Your wife's sitting here next to me. We're in my car. Talk to her."

He thrust the phone at her. She pushed the hair out of her eyes, her voice warm and anxious.

"Dougal? It's me, darling."

Weber's fingers closed on hers, retrieving the instrument. "Make sure your friend hears what I'm saying. We can all come out of this safely, Macneil. I'm offering you a deal. Did you come in by boat?"

The Canadian's hesitation proved that the colonel's hunch was right. Macneil cleared his throat.

"Let me talk to my wife again."

She was as close to Weber as she could be without touching him, straining her ears to hear.

"That'll have to wait," Weber said curtly. "Are you listening?"

He heard a thud as if the other car had hit the curb. Macneil's voice was suddenly loud.

"I'm listening."

Weber's lips were close to the mouthpiece. "I'm leaving Montoro with you. That's the deal. That and the films against your wife. You've got five seconds to make up your mind."

The surf boomed a short hundred yards away. For a moment he thought the line had gone dead. Then Macneil came on again.

"How can I be sure this is on the level, Weber?"

209

"You can't," the colonel answered. "You've got to take me on trust. It's your only chance to see your wife again alive. Where's your boat?"

Macneil's voice cracked. "Palo Island. It's off the bluff near Paláu's house. There's a dinghy under the trees."

Weber's smile was unconscious. It was the one place obvious and yet he had missed it.

"Where are you now — your exact position?"

There was a muttered consultation before Macneil answered. "Two blocks behind P.I.D.E. headquarters, facing north."

The smile faded. They hadn't been that far behind him. "Wait there for fifteen minutes," Weber ordered. "Then drive to the bluff. I'll be waiting for you. Flash your headlamps when you get there. Bring the films with you — all of them, the negatives too. And listen, get rid of your friend."

He lowered the armrest on the radiophone. There was nothing to fear from Zuimárraga. The general lost a police chief but he kept his image. It would be easy enough to account for the colonel's disappearance.

Weber's shoulders lifted. "It's up to him now," he said stonily.

The windows were down. A warm breeze came off the ocean, linking them with another continent. The Mercedes climbed back onto the hardtop, the rear wheels showering sand. He watched the speedometer needle climb into the nineties and held it there. The telephone poles flicked by like the accusing fingers of the dead.

"You *couldn't* be lying now." It was no more than a whisper but he heard.

The years had left him indifferent to sentiment and criticism alike. Yet the girl's question both angered and disturbed him. Somehow he couldn't bring himself to answer.

DOUGAL MACNEIL

HE WAS WATCHING the dashboard clock. Eleven of the fifteen minutes had gone. Zuimárraga was breathing heavily beside him.

"Weber will keep his word."

Macneil looked at him impassively. Zuimárraga's tone was almost encouraging. The general's expression grew uneasy. The clock hands edged into the last seconds. Macneil nodded.

"All right, let's go."

Zuimárraga switched on the ignition. "Aren't you going to let me out?"

Macneil shook his head. "You're coming with me."

Zuimárraga's fat face was the color of putty. "I know this man — he said alone. You cannot afford to play with him."

Macneil's jaw muscles tightened. "I'm not playing with anyone. Now get this thing moving."

Colored streaks traced the sky over the city. Macneil saw nothing but the ribbon of black unwinding in front of them. He was thinking of the village where he had lived. They were simple enough memories — crab-fishing from the bedroom windows — the lottery of the day's mail —

walks along the beach with Pilar. Her face seemed to grow before him, blotting out everything else. Part of what they had had together was lost forever. He looked at the man behind the wheel with fresh bitterness.

The suspension bridge showed up ahead, a single silver span reaching into the darkness. He sat up straighter, watching for the post that marked the cutoff to the bluff. Zuimárraga sent the car bumping down the track between the savannah pines. Macneil touched his arm.

"Hold it!" Mosquitoes whined in through the open window. They were twenty yards from the spot where he'd tied up the dinghy. A night bird's call drifted across from the jungle side of the river. Moonlight covered the dark-green water. Alligators lay on the sandspits like fallen logs. Their musty odor was discernible even at this distance. The eastern tip of the island was a hundred yards or so away. Macneil gestured behind him.

"In the back. Lie flat on the floor."

They looked at one another for a long minute. Then the general climbed over awkwardly. He knelt behind, his head showing above the seat. His face was shiny with sweat.

"If he sees me, he'll kill me."

Macneil stretched out and pushed the other's head down. He flashed the headlamps twice. The beam lit the trees on the island. Suddenly the dinghy appeared. Weber's powerful shoulders were to the shore, pulling the dinghy with long powerful strokes. Macneil slipped the gun into the glove compartment. His only hope was to play this straight. A sense of injustice made his voice harsh and angry. "Why don't you go on back to confession. It's your day not ours."

A cloud of whining mosquitoes followed him to the edge of the water. He climbed onto the mangrove roots and called. Weber turned the dinghy so that he faced the bank. He shipped the oars, training his gun at Macneil. The Canadian grabbed a branch, displaying the yellow folder in his free hand. The current brought Weber directly underneath.

The German looked up. "Drop it in the boat!"

Macneil let the folder fall. Weber riffed through the contents. He held the dinghy steady as Macneil climbed down. Weber's teeth were a slash of white.

"You row."

He sat facing, the photographs in his lap. Macneil leaned into his stroke, digging the blades in deep. The dinghy pulled away from the shore. Something moved on the bank behind Weber's back. It was Zuimárraga, pushing his way through the trailing greenery. His face was stone-carved in the moonlight. He raised the gun deliberately, his left hand gripping his right wrist. Macneil's shout of warning was instinctive. Weber came to his feet, swinging around in the rocking boat. The cry never left his brain. The shot plowed into his head above his ear. Zuimárraga fired twice more but Weber was already dead. He pitched slowly sideways reaching out as if diving. The stream caught his body, whirling it away, face down. The yellow folder floated behind on the bloodstained surface.

The echoes of the shots cracked like wet sails. They fired back at the island, died in the wooded bluff behind. An alligator flopped from a sandbank, eyes and snout

214

showing in the quicksilver water. Undertow had swept the body beyond the eastern tip of the island. The alligator changed its course to meet the corpse. There was nothing to see or hear — nothing but the memory of Weber erect, a puzzled look in his dark eyes.

Macneil righted the dinghy. Headlamps stabbed through the trees. The car raced away, whining at high speed as it hit the marginal highway. He pulled toward the island mechanically. The oars splintered his palms but he felt nothing. He was calling Pilar's name long before he reached the mouth of the creek. She stumbled toward him as he stepped onto the landing stage. Her cheeks were puffed with mosquito bites. She looked up at him, tracing the outline of his eyes and mouth with her fingertips.

"The shots," she whispered.

He held her close. "Zuimárraga killed Weber. There was nothing I could do." He fought the returning wave of revulsion.

She lifted herself on her toes, gripping him by the shoulders.

"I love you, Dougal."

It was the only thing that mattered. He unfastened her hands gently.

"The tide's on the turn. We've got to run for it."

The screen of eucalyptus branches had been stripped from the cabin cruiser. He took her bag from the cabin and helped her. She leaned against the side of the cockpit, nose pinched, her dark hair soaked with sweat.

"I'll be all right," she said weakly. "Just don't look at me — leave me alone."

He cast off and hit the starting button. The sudden clatter of the diesel was loud in the creek. He steered out into midstream keeping wide of the sandbanks. She was crying softly. He pulled a canvas chair close to the wheel and made her sit in it. Her back was pressed against his leg. The island was already out of sight. He hugged the jungle shore, the throttle wide open. The bows lifted as they reached the mouth of the estuary. He altered his course to north by northwest, fixing his eyes on the horizon. Two more miles and they'd be out of danger. It was almost three o'clock. Ribbons of false dawn lit the sky. He took his hands off the wheel, feeling her shaking. He bent down, soothing her distress.

"What is it?"

She shook her head miserably, her damp hair falling over her eyes.

"Weber. I can't get it out of my mind. No one should die like that — it's wrong!"

"Is there a right way of dying?" he asked. He lifted her head and kissed her on the mouth. "Try not to think about it."

He brought the boat back on course. The night wind was warm on his face. There was nothing now between them and Puerto Vedra but the sea.

≫≫ If you've enjoyed this book and would like to discover more great vintage crime and thriller titles, as well as the most exciting crime and thriller authors writing today, visit: ≫≫

The Murder Room
Where Criminal Minds Meet

themurderroom.com